James Davie Butler

Butleriana, Genealogica et Biographica

Or Genealogical Notes Concerning Mary Butler and Her Descendants...

James Davie Butler

Butleriana, Genealogica et Biographica
Or Genealogical Notes Concerning Mary Butler and Her Descendants...

ISBN/EAN: 9783337031206

Printed in Europe, USA, Canada, Australia, Japan

Cover: Foto ©Raphael Reischuk / pixelio.de

More available books at **www.hansebooks.com**

BUTLERIANA,

GENEALOGICA ET BIOGRAPHICA;

OR

Genealogical notes concerning

MARY BUTLER

AND HER DESCENDANTS, AS WELL AS THE BATES, HARRIS,
SIGOURNEY AND OTHER FAMILIES, WITH WHICH
THEY HAVE INTERMARRIED.

BY

JAMES DAVIE BUTLER.

In Memoriam Majorum, Ubi numerantur avorum.

ALBANY, N. Y.
JOEL MUNSELL'S SONS, PUBLISHERS.
1888

CONTENTS.

ILLUSTRATIONS.

PREFACE.

" Honor thy Father and thy Mother."

Whoever writes his father's name on his fath
tombstone is an incipient genealogist. He sho
the germ of a feeling which, if it could, would writ
indelibly the names of all his progenitors, even back
to his first father. He is therefore guilty of incon-
sistency, if he hems in his genealogical interest by
the record in his ancestral Bible or by family tradition. Moreover, he who forgets the past has no
claim to be remembered by the future.

Our public records are not without genealogical
value, and we should make the most of them. But
it cannot be enough regretted that regarding lineage
they are so far inferior to those of a neighbor we
are prone to despise. In the Canadian Bureau of
Archives "the merest peasant finds the complete
record of his family history, extending back to the
ancestor who left his hamlet in the old France to seek
a home in the wilds of the new France. As one
stands before the cases that contain the three hundred
manuscript volumes of which this remarkable work

is composed, each volume labeled and ready for the
printer, a feeling of admiration must arise for a
people who can leave to posterity such monuments
of its individual life."

Only one of my connections,—a Sigourney,—
has published anything concerning our lineage.
Material for it is scanty and scattered. Just for
this reason have I felt it incumbent on me to gather
the fragments that were dropping out of sight and
out of mind, as well as to put them in charge of
the art preservative of all arts. Thus I would fain
garner up such knowledge of our family past as
may help forecast the future, or at least serve as a
stepping-stone to further research.

This work was commenced in September, 1839,
while the writer was a student in Andover. Aside
from Family Records in Bibles, the details first
secured were mainly derived from ancient registers
concerning births, marriages and deaths then preserved in manuscript in the Old State House,
Boston. In this way the Butler lineage was traced
up to the birth of the first-born of Stephen, Aug. 2,
1653. Further than this it seemed impossible to
go. In 1847 the New England *Historical and Genealogical Register* published, in its April number, an
outline of whatever particulars had been up to that
time discovered. It was not till thirteen years afterward that I learned that the mother of Stephen
Butler was named Mary,—and that in his childhood she was married to a second husband, Benjamin Ward. For these facts as well as for a copy

of her will, I was indebted to a total stranger, Andrew H. Ward of West Newton, a favor I shall never forget.

My mother's father, Israel Harris (505) survived till I was twenty-one years old, and I often met him. My genealogical tastes were, however, still in embryo, and when they began to develop I soon ascertained that no one of his descendants could inform me either where he was born, or the christian name of his father. Most people called that name Timothy or Israel. In fact it was John. This true name, however, remained hid from me till 1886, largely because I had grown up in the belief that my grand-father's birth had been in Sharon, Conn., and when convinced by Gen. Sedgwick that this notion was a mistake, I was taught by him to look for what I sought in Nine Partners, Duchess Co., N. Y. The true birth-place Cornwall, first came to my knowledge when I obtained the pension claim of Israel Harris (505) from Washington. Nor was I able to trace the Harris lineage-line back of Israel's father until the year 1888.

Minutiae regarding earliest ancestors have been chronicled, so far as possible, either as curious, or characteristic, or in the hope that these small handles would help at length to draw greater things out "of the dark backward and abysm of time." Similar is my reason for inserting wills and various public documents. In a dark night the faintest gleam has its value.

In this book that which is wanting cannot be

numbered. But it embodies the gleanings of a half
century. It garners up fragments which could not
now,—all of them,—be gathered by any painstaking
no matter how great. It will give a sort of van-
tage-ground for further research to others after me
who shall consider the days of old and apply themselves to the search of their fathers. I am only
sorry that I know no one among my kin or kith
who, as a critic, has earned the right to throw the
first stone at me, by giving a tithe of the attention
which I have given to our family genealogy. To
those observant of the strong connections and nice
dependences of heredity and kindred, my endeavors
will not seem to have been wasted.

Notices of corrections or additions which may
occur to readers will be very welcome to the author.

                              JAMES DAVIE BUTLER.
MADISON, WISCONSIN, MAY, 1888.

ABBREVIATIONS, ETC.

ca. = *circa,* about.

et sqq = and following pages.

M. R. Massachusetts Records.

Gen. Reg. New England Historical and Genealogical Register.

R. C. = Record Commissioners of Boston.

The syllable " bis " attached to a number indicates that there was some reason for repeating the same number, somewhere in the series.

Savage = Genealogical Dictionary of the first settlers of New England.

Sedg = Sedgwick's History of Sharon, Conn.

S. H. = State House of Massachusetts.

Where several persons bear the same name they are distinguished by numbers [1] [2] [3] etc., at the right of each name.

The numbers at the left-hand of the names indicating the first mention of each, do not form an unbroken series. It was not convenient to make them so, and it was not necessary.

The numbers at the right hand of names and in parentheses, refer back to the earliest mention of those names.

MARY BUTLER.

Concerning *Mary Butler*, my ancestress, the earliest fact known is that she was living in Boston in the year 1635. On January 11, 1637-8, twelve acres of land north-west of Muddy River were confirmed to her second husband Benjamin Ward, by the authorities, and their bounds defined. This land seems to have been allotted to him on Dec. 14, 1635. In a list of 52 persons to whom "great allotments" were then voted his name stands second. (R. C., 2nd Rept., p. 22.)

Mrs. Butler had become a widow long before, with one child, named Stephen. About the year 1621 she was married to Benjamin Ward. By this second marriage she had one child, a daughter Mary.

Not far from 1652 this daughter became the wife of William Holloway who had come from Marshfield or Taunton in 1650.

The children were :

1. Mary, b. 1653, April 2.
2. William, b. 1654-5, Jan. 11, m. Decline.
3. Benjamin, b. 1656, July 8, m. 1682, Mary Stocker. The three were all living in 1667. •

BENJAMIN WARD.

The following short and simple annals have been gleaned from various sources.

1640, June 6. Benjamin Ward with Mary his wife united with the church in Boston.

1641, June 2. In a list of 126 persons who were then "made free" the name of Benjamin Ward is No 104. (Mass. Records, Vol. I. p. 379.)

According to Memorial History of Boston (Vol. II. p. xli.) one acre on the marshy shore was granted to Benjamin Ward. It may have been given him because he was a shipwright, for shipwrights were exempt from taxation, (Idem I. 498) and Ward may have been one of the six sent by the London company to Massachusetts Bay in 1629. (General Reg. xxv. p. 7) So, in the Book of Possessions 1645— which is made up of the original entries of the earliest recorded divisions of land (R. C. No. 46. p. 107) we read : " B. Ward (G. 103) one house and about one acre on the north side of Fort Hill, and south of the marsh."

In 1647, April 26, "Liberty was granted him to wharf before his own property."

1648, Feb. 26. "There was granted to Benjamin Ward, Stephen Butler [this is the earliest mention I have discovered of the name Butler] and six others liberty to make a highway from their houses over the marsh to the bridge, upon their own charges which were £8—16s., for which outlay they are free from highway charges this nine years." In 1648, he rented "one eighth of the town marsh, 12½ rods fronting on the water, joining his former land and workhouse, to the south east, paying £3 annually for the use and benefit of the free schools of Boston." (Suffolk Deeds, Vol. III. p. 454.)

In 1649 Bejamin Ward had bound himself to pay sixpence per acre annual rent for his land at Long Island [in the Harbor.] (R. C. 2nd Rept. p. 95).

In 1657, John Martin was made freeman, Benjamin Ward giving a bond of £20 to secure the town from any charges for him. (Ibid, p. 142). In 1638 "a house plott" had been granted Martin as a "ship carpenter." A fac simile of the name Benjamin Ward is given in the Memorial History of Boston. (Vol. II. p. xli) In 1651 he served as a juryman. He died in 1666. On Dec. 26 of that year his widow was appointed his administratrix.

PETITION AND WILL OF MARY BUTLER WARD.

The following official documents were printed in the New England *Hist. and Genealogical Register* (Vol. XVIII. pp. 154-6) and were derived from the Suffolk County Probate Records. Manuscript copies of them I had procured long before :

1666 Dec. 26.

At a meeting of the Govr. Major Generall and Recorder, Power of Administration to the Estate of the late *Benjamin Ward*, shipwright, deceased, is granted to *Mary*, his relict, shee bringing in an inventory of that estate to the next County Court, and giving security to Administer thereupon according to Law.   EDW. RAWSON, Record^r.

During the life-time of Benjamin Ward he had assured friends that his two sons Stephen Butler

and William Halloway "did agree very well." But
when Ward died intestate, Holloway who had married Ward's daughter was disposed to deprive Butler
of any share in the Ward estate. Hence Butler's
mother, Mary Ward, was led to petition the authorities that one-half of her husband's property might
be given to her, and remain at her disposal. Antic-
ipating that her request would be granted, as in
truth it was, though after her death, she made a
will bequeathing half her husband's estate, which
was inventoried at £940, to Stephen Butler, and the
other half to the Holloways. She took this course,
as she says, "judging it for peace sake, and that
my son and son-in-law and grandchildren may live
in love and peace." Her will was legalized by the
government, but was not executed without great
delay and difficulty.

Her measures for obtaining control over the Ward
property are described in the following Public Documents :

(S. H. Sec. State's office. Docs. 1622–1700, 13, 15, 237.)

May 18, 1667.

Mary Ward—Petition.

To the Honorable the General Court now assem-
bled. The humble petition of Mary Ward, Widdow—Humbly Showeth :

That it hath pleased God lately to take to him-
selfe the late *Benjamin Ward*, youre Petitioner's
deare Husband, before hee did, or could, settle that
estate which God hath bestowed on him, by his and

your Petitioner's labor and care for about Forty and five years, wherein they lived together with the constant and faithful service of *Stephen Butler*, sonn to the Petitioner by a former husband, who was very deare to your Petitioner's late Husband, Ward, who always told your petitioner, that hee resolved to manifest his love and affection to her said sonn Butler, as to his own that God had given to themselves, as a reward of all his faithful and dilligent service both before and after he was for himself, but hee dying intestate and youre Petitioner very aged and weake and unfit to manage what is left, and being desirous that the Estate of her late Husband may be divided and settled on herselfe and her three grandchildren, which is all the issue that God hath pleased to spare the Petitioner and her late Husband, the one half thereof to your petitioner and her dispose, whereby shee may be enabled to live in some measure comfortably the remainder of her life, but also leave behind her some Testimony of her love to her sonn Butler and his children to whom her Husband intended so well. And the other halfe of the whole to her said grand-children, to be given to them at the day of marriage, and youre Petitioner as in duty bound shall pray.

In answer to the Petition of Mary Ward, Widdow, the Court on Perusal of the Petition, declare that the Cognizance thereof belongs to the County Court of Suffolk, to whom it is referred.

EDW. RAWSON,
Secretary.

Trusting her petition would in due time be granted, as in fact it was, Mrs. Ward lost no time in
drawing up the following WILL:

I, Mary Ward, Relict of the late *Benjamin Ward*,
of Boston, being weake of body, but of perfect un-
derstanding, Considering the trouble I have met with
and been put unto, by reason sickness came so on,
and death suddenly issuing, taking my Husband out
of this world before hee settled his Estate and know-
ing that he often declared unto me that having from
a child brought up my sonn *Stephen Butler* that I
had by a former Husband, that he found so dutiful,
hopeful and serviceable to him as if he had been his
owne, hee alwayes telling me hee minded to give
him a considerable part of his land and Estate, that
had so great a hand in and helping to gett it, least
after my decease my dear Husband's mind should
not be understood, I having alwayes a hand also in
getting of the Estate, judge it for peace sake, that
my sonn and sonn-in-Lawe and grandchildren may
live in love and peace,—necessary to make this my
last will and Testament, being sole Administratrix
to my late Husband's Estate, hereby annulling any
late or former will of mine.

I give to my Reverend Pastor Mr *John Wilson*
40s; [He was pastor of the First church, which stood
in State Street on the site of Brazer's Building. His
death was 1667 Aug. 7.] to Mr *Thacher* and Mr *Allen*
40s a peece; to the Poore of the church of Boston
Four pounds. To my sonn in lawe William Hol-

loway Tenn pounds. Unto my much Honored Friends Major Generall *John Leverett* and Mr *Peter Olliver*, my Ancient and neere neighbors alwayes helpfull to me Thee [Three] pounds a peece, to buy them a ring.

I bequeath all the rest of my Estate both reall and personall, in Houses, Landes, wharfes, goods and Household stuffe and whatsoever my Husband left and I now possess, the one halfe thereof, that is . of all the Houses, Lands and goods to my three grandchildren, *Mary Holloway* whom my Husband and I brought up, *William Holloway* and *Benjamin Holloway* to be divided Equally between them when they come to be of age, and that they bee heires each to other.

And in Case of their decease, the one halfe to their Father *William Holloway* and the other halfe to *Stephen Butler*, my sonn and his heirs.

I give the other halfe of the Houses, Lands, and goods to my beloved sonn *Stephen Butler* and his children, he having soe industriously laboured with and for my Husband, and in case of his and all his childrens decease, before my grand-children being of age, in such Case, what I give to them my mind and will is that it should goe to my grand-children, or the longest liver of them.

My will is that my son in law *William Holloway* shall give security to my Executor to Render it up what I have given to my grandchildren, that during their non-age he shall have the benefit and improvement thereof. I appoint my son *Stephen Butler* to bee sole Executor of this my last will and Testament, and desire my Honored Friends Major General *John Leverett* and Mr *Peter Olliver* to be overseers of the same.

MARY + WARD.

4 July 1667.

In presence of us

William Salter, Henry Allen, John Prince, John Saunders.

That making a mark instead of signing a name was no clear proof of ignorance of writing has been well shown in Gen. Reg. (Vol. XLI. p. 95). Yet Shakespeare's daughter but a decade or two older than Mrs. Ward, could not write.

21 July 1667.

William Salter and *Henry Allen* deposed :

The testimony of *Henry Allen* aged 47 years or thereabouts, testifieth and saith that having conference with Brother *Ward* deceased, not long before his death, concerning the disposall of his estate, and to my best remembrance that he did answer mee that it should be divided amongst them, and that his sons did carry on the work together, as witnes my hand.

Deposed in County Court 31 July, 1667 ; by *Henry Allen* as Attests.

EDW. RAWSON, Record^r.

The testimony of *Richard Gridley*, aged 65 years: Testifieth and saith that having had conference with Brother *Ward*, deceased, about 2 years since, hearing him Complaine of the trouble hee had with his servants, I did ask him how he did Carry on his work now. And he did Answer mee that hee was Eased of his trouble by his two sonns, for they did Carry on the work Comfortably, and that they did agree very well, and then I did ask of him how hee did think to dispose of his Estate lying as it did abroad and at home, hee did tell me that the better they did, the better it should bee for them, for it should be divided together, for they did each one the worke to his great Comfort.

his marke
RICHARD × GRIDLEY.

Sworn to in Court by *Richard Gridley.*

EDW. RAWSON, Record^r.

At a County Court held at Boston, 31 July, 1667: The Court on due perusall of the late Mary Ward's Petition to the Generall Court in May last, and the Court's answer thereunto, with the evidences of *Richard Gridley* and *Henry Allen*, together with the last will and Testament of the said *Mary Ward*, now also proved in this Court by sufficient evidences to be her last will and Testament, considering her equal minde and due Care to her Children both by her first and second Husband, doe allow and confirme the said will to bee a fynall issue for the

settling of the Estate between the children, order-
ing that her Petition and evidences therewith bee
recorded with that her will.

EDW. RAWSON, Record'.

1667, Nov. 12. Report of Benj. Gillam and others
appointed to make a division of Ward's estate.
(B. 15, 31) and Nov. 17, 1667, B. 15, 237.

STEPHEN BUTLER.

On Dec. 21, 1667, the estate of Mary Ward was
divided between her two sons by probate appointees
S. H. ; B. 15, 108-110.   Holloway being dissatisfied with the division, petitioned the General Court
for an alteration.   These authorities, at their session
in April, 1668, permitted him " to take his choice
of either part of the division." (M. R., iv, 384 p.)
Butler was dissatisfied, having made improvements
on his portion (M. R., iv, 332 p.), and was by the
next General Court reinstated in what the Probate
Court had assigned him.   Holloway kept up the
controversy till his death, and then his children
carried it on at least till 1686.   The decisions of the
General Court, in what they called "a troublesome
case," were all in favor of Butler.   In 1681-2, March
17, as Holloway had deceased, his children were
ordered to pay Butler £200 or at least £150 (p. 356)
New England currency (M. R., vol. v, p. 340).   In
1683 (v, 416) "execution was ordered against the
    2

housing they lived in " if they were not prompt to pay. Papers relating to this matter are in State House, Sec. of State's office, vol. xvi, pp. 38, 91, 187, 265, 286, 386 90, vol. xxxix, 652, 699, vol. xl, p. 228.

The other mentions I find of Stephen Butler are these : In 1663, a highway not less than fifteen feet in breadth was ordered run through land in his possession by the sea. (R. C., 50, p. 77.) In 1673 it had cost him £8 16s., and its breadth was made twelve feet towards the bridge by the corner of the Blue Bell, and extended to a wharf formerly Benjamin Ward's. In 1675 he and Wm. Holloway were ordered by referees to set up a fence which they had plucked down.

In Boston indexed documents, vol. 69, p. 131, June 7, 1667, Stephen Butler petitions for release from imprisonment.

Stephen Butler was a soldier in King Philip's war. In 1675, Aug. 12, as a soldier in Capt. Lathrop's company, he was charged at Hatfield 1s. 9d., for a pouch and belt, being one of 13 members of the same company who were furnished with supplies at the same time. On the 18th of the next month, Sept., 71 persons of that company were killed by Indians at Muddy Brook. On Dec. 10th of the same year, his name appears among the troops under Maj. Appleton, and he was credited as having £3, 18s., then his due. About a week afterward, Dec. 19, this force stormed the strongest fort of the Narragansetts. (Gen. Reg., vol. xxxviii, pp. 338, 444) the hardest fight in the war ; 80 whites were killed and 150 wounded. In 1688-9, Feb. 13, for £100 he and wife Tabitha mortgaged to Margaret Thacher, land near the brick house formerly belonging to Benj. Ward. 1695, is the last year in which I find mention of Stephen Butler. At that date his name appears in a list of Bostonians among the inhabitants of the seventh ward. (R. C. Doc., 92, p. 159.) His son James had already been six years dead.

TRADITIONARY ORIGIN.

According to John O'Hart (Irish Pedigrees, p. 242) " The ancestors of the Butlers came from Normandy to England with William the Conqueror. Their original name was Fitz-Walter, from Walter one of their ancestors ; and Theobald Fitz-Walter came to Ireland with Henry the Second in 1172 and had the office of Chief Butler of Ireland conferred on him, the [duty attached to which was to attend at the coronation of the kings of England, and present them with the first cup of wine. From the office of Butlership of Ireland they took the name of " Butler."

In the reign of Edward the Third, Tipperary was formed into the "county palatine of Ormond" under the Butlers, who thus became so powerful that different branches of them furnished many of the most distinguished families in Ireland. " The Palatine possesssed such royal privileges that he ruled in his Palatinate almost as a king. The Butlers were earls, marquises and dukes of Ormond, and also had the following titles in Tipperary: earls of Carrick, earls of Glengall, viscounts of Thurles, viscounts of Skerrin and barons of Cahir." " In the reign of Henry VIII, they gained possession of a great part of Carlow " (p. 294). " The county Kilkenny became possessed mostly by the Butlers, earls of Ormond " (p. 304). They were called earls of Ossory, and Gowran, viscounts of

Galway, and various other titles derived from their extensive estates." (305 p.) Their war-cry was *Butler Aboo!* the word Aboo is the old Celtic for Victory (p. 348).

The word *Ormond* is said to mean in Irish East Munster. According to "The Norman People"—a London volume of 1874 (p. 182) the Ormond family, through the Irish chief butler, is traceable to a Walter who came over with the Conqueror, and in 1086 was owner of estates in Lailand, Lancashire. This Walter came from Glanville near Caen. His arms were a chief indented.

It is an inveterate tradition in divers families of American Butlers that they are descended from collateral branches of the family of James Butler, the Duke of Ormond (1610—1688.) Thus, Dr. Geo. H. Butler of N. Y., writes regarding his ancestor Thomas Butler born about 1674. "Although it has never been questioned, and there is no doubt of its truth, yet in the absence of the exact date of his birth and of parish records, positive proof of his descent from the house of Ormond, and of his right to the following blazonry, viz :

Arms, Or, a chief indented azure;

Crest, in a ducal coronet, or, a plume of five ostrich feathers;

Ar, a falcon rising out of the last, is impossible."

Notwithstanding this impossibility, the Doctor sets this beautiful escutcheon in the fore-front of his excellent work regarding his family lineage. Thomas Butler above-mentioned was an early

settler in the Province of Maine, but a similar claim
of kindred with the noble house of Ormond is made
by the descendants of James Butler, an Irishman,
who died in Woburn near Boston, Jan. 20, 1681.
One of these claimants was asking among other
things, of a recent emigrant whether the Butlers
did not still stand high in Ireland. The answer
was: "Yes indeed, sir, I have seen some of them
stand so high *that they stood on nothing whatever.*"

This Woburn James Butler who is said to have
been brought to America when a child of four years,
may have been a kinsman of this Boston family of
Butlers of which I write, and from him they may
have adopted the name James. At all events the
members of that Boston branch have from time
immemorial asserted their Ormond relationship.
We find the name James among them in every
generation.

Nor is the aspiration to Ormond kinship confined
to Americans. We find it in John Butler, captain
in the 55th Bengal Regiment, who in 1845 published
in Sibsagor, Assam, "Memoranda" on his Butler
ancestors. He describes Walter, a young Ormond,
according to tradition, leaving Kilkenny, and settled
in Hampshire, before 1628. He became a land-
holder some fifty miles west of London, and his
acres were transmitted down generation after generation to his posterity, whose line is traced by the
captain even in the present century.

These pretensions may be all equally true, or
equally false, but whether each countenances or

discredits the others, and whether to call them true or false, we have as yet no means of deciding.

That the father of Stephen, my earliest known ancestor, should turn out to have been the cousin or brother of Walter just mentioned, would be nothing surprising. If that father was killed in an Irish battle, as our family tradition asserts, it would have been natural for his widow to fly with her child and take refuge with Walter, the relative in Hants. Hants is a maritime county and therefore one of those where we must look for the Old World home of Benjamin Ward, the shipwright. There too the young Irish widow may naturally have met her future husband.

SUMMARY OF BUTLER LINEAGE.

1. Mary Butler (Ward) in Boston, 1635.
2. Her son Stephen, b. in 1620 ca., m. Mary Jane and Tabitha.
7. Their son James, b. 1665, m. Grace Newcomb.
17. Their son James, b. 1688, m. Abigail Eustiss.
24. Their son James, b. 1713, m. Elizabeth Davie. (5 D.)
25. Their son James, b. 1720, m. Mary Sigourney. (822.)
28. Their son James D., b. 1765, m. Rachel Harris. (511.)
41. Their son James D., b. 1815, m. Anna Bates. (334.)
82. Their son James D., b. 1846, m. Sarah Adamson. (after No. 87.)

THE BUTLER LINEAGE THROUGH TEN GENERATIONS.

FIRST GENERATION.

1. Mary Butler with her son Stephen came to Boston as early as 1635. She was then the wife of Benjamin Ward to whom she had been married more than ten years, and had borne him Mary, their only child. Her death was in July 1667.

SECOND GENERATION AND CHILDREN.

2. Stephen Butler of Boston m. Jane ——, Mary and Tabitha. He d. 1695 ca.

His children by Jane were:

3. Benjamin, b. 1653 Aug. 2, d. an infant.
4. Benjamin, b. 1658 Feb. 10, m. Susanna Gallup.
5. Isaac, b. 1661 Oct. 9, d. an infant.
6. Isaac, b. 1664 May 29, d. an infant.
7. James¹, b. 1665 Aug. 2, m. Grace Newcomb.
8. Isaac, b. 1667 Aug. 10, m. Tabitha Sewall.

The children of Stephen B.(2) by his wife Mary were:

9. William¹, b. 1671 Oct. 10.
10. Susanna, m. Seavey.

The children of Stephen Butler (2) by his wife Tabitha, dau. of John Blower, were:

9 bis. Stephen, b. 1681 April 22.

10 bis. Tabitha, b. 1687 June 16.

Both their names (9 bis and 10 bis) appear Aug. 1, 1715, in an agreement with Samuel Sewall regarding a passage-way.

Tabitha Butler was alive in 1715.

THIRD GENERATION AND CHILDREN.

Benjamin Butler (4) m. 1676 Mar. 7 Susanna Gallup).

Their daughter

12. Susan Butler, Dec. 13, 1699, m. John Loring.

13. James Butler (7) m. Grace Newcombe, dau. of Andrew N., mariner. He d. 1689. She was born 1664 Oct. 10.

Their children were:

14. Mary², b. 168³ Feb. 16, m. Francis Brock 1698 July 29.

15. Grace, b. 1685 May 2, m. Thomas Jackson.

16. Elizabeth¹, b. 1686 Dec. 23, m. Savage?

17. James², b. 1688 Aug. 21, m. Abigail Eustiss.

The second husband of Grace Newcomb Butler was Andrew Rankin, m. 1692 April 15. Their son Andrew was b. 1693 July 13.

The children of Susannah Butler (12) and John Loring were:

Susanna, b. 1700 Oct. 15.

12 bis, Joseph.

13 bis, Rachel.

14 bis, Nathaniel.

15 bis, Thomas.

3

William Butler (9) m. Mary Greenleaf.
Their only child was :
16 bis. Thomas.

William Butler (9) 1703 Dec. 9 m. Mary Shepcot.

The Will of (v) shipwright, March 15, 1713–14, appoints as executors his widow and Stephen Greenleaf. Leaves wife sole use of his estate till Thomas comes of age, afterward one-half the estate, and the whole in case of son's death. William B. recovered Ward lands that on Feb. 13, 1688–9, had been mortgaged for £100 by his father Stephen.

Concerning James Butler (13) I have met with the following notices.

Born in 1665, he may have been the James Butler who in 1675, was servant, that is apprentice to John Keen, who, for a dozen years after, was a prominent man in Boston. (R. C. Doc., 92, pp. 46, 48).

In 1683-4 Jan. 28, James Butler [and another] became surety to the town for Matthew Maberly, a spoon-maker and his family (R. C. Doc., 150, p. 74.) In 1681 he is set down as taxed in the district of Major Savage, collector. In Oct. 1683, 10, James Butler in prison for selling liquor petitions for release. State Archives, xi, 121. In 1684 he, or another James Butler, was licensed to keep a tavern. (R. C. Doc. 50, p. 71.) In 1687 was taxed 21s, on a valuation of £24 for what is termed "4 Housing" ; 25 persons were assessed at

a less tax ; 30 at more and 8 at the same. His
father, Stephen Butler, was at the same time taxed
the same amount on four houses, mills and
wharves. (R. C. Doc., 92, p. 108.)

His residence was on the south side of Fort Hill
which was in the southerly part of Boston. He
dying in 1689 at the age of 24 years, his widow
Grace, on Aug. 29, 1689, was appointed administratrix of the estate of her late husband, James
Butler, shipwright, intestate. On the same day
an inventory of his property by John Wing and
Edward Browne was exhibited in the Probate
Court and sworn to by the administratrix, amounting to £300, 15s.

Among the items were the following :

Plate and coin . . .	£37 10s.
Negro boy and girl . . .	£30.
House and land in Boston . .	£88.
House, barn and land in Worcester.	£46.
Musket and arms . . .	£1 10s.

Previous to 1682, forty acres of land had been
allotted him in Worcester.

The following incident deserves commemoration
as a proof that tradition is often more trustworthy
than many suppose. This James Butler, according
to my father who heard the story more than a
century ago, would never taste pork, because it re-
minded him of the odor brought to him by the
wind as, when a boy, he had seen a woman burned
at the stake on Boston Common. This report long
seemed incredible, yet when he was sixteen years

old a negress was really burnt there Sept. 22, 1681.
(Mass. Hist. Soc. Proceedings, 1855 8, p. 320.) This
scrap of history was strangely saved from oblivion.
In 1858 the only surviving child of Jeremy Belknap presented her father's papers to the Massachusetts Historical Society. A committee appointed to examine them, found numerous MS.
extracts which had been copied by Belknap from a
diary of Cotton Mather, a work long supposed to
have perished. The last of the extracts which they
decided to print ran thus : "1681, Sept. 22. A
negro woman who burnt two houses in Roxbury,
July 12, in one of which a child was burnt to death,
was executed in Boston. She was burnt to death,
the first that has suffered such a death in New
England."

Isaac Butler (8) ca 1687 m. Tabitha Sewall. (Sewall, Vol II, p. 414.)

18. Their son Stephen m. 1708 May 27, Joanna
Bennett b. 1688, Jan. 7, d, 1714, Jan. 3.

Their dau. was Mary.

Stephen (18) had a second wife Mary, perhaps
sister of his first. He was a blacksmith. (See
Suffolk Wills, 19, 145, 175.) In 1715, Aug. 1, he
was witness to an agreement of Samuel Sewall as
to a passage way. His wife Mary survived him.

FOURTH GENERATION AND THEIR CHILDREN.

Grace Butler (15) 1706, Dec. 26, m. Thomas Jackson son of John and Elizabeth. She d. 1759, March

James Butler

His Book

James

1713

James Butler junr — Bible Boston March 13

1752

the above Butler jr son

15. The ceremony was performed by Benjamin Wadsworth, Pastor of the 1st Church.

Their children were :

19. Grace, b. 1708. Aug. 30.

20. Thomas, b. 1709, Feb. 19.

21. Elizabeth, b, 1711, Dec. 7.·

In 1727-8 at the request of the three children of James Butler who had died. Thomas Jackson was appointed their guardian and continued in that trust till Jan 30, 1734-5. His Bible shows the name "James Butler (17) his Book, 1713" written in a better hand than any of his posterity can boast. (See illustration.) Its price 40s is marked on the first fly-leaf. On the death of its owner in 1715, it passed into the hands of his sister Grace Jackson. At her death, March 15, 1759, it was received by the above Butler's grandson. James Butler Jr., (25) b. 1739-40, who kept it till his death in 1827, when it was transmitted to his son James Davie (28). From him it passed on his death in 1842, to a second James Davie (41), whose son, bearing the same name (82), on his twentieth birthday June 25, 1866, inscribed his name in the same sacred book.

This Bible is folio, printed at London in 1690, with brief notes by Samuel Clark, b. 1626, a Cambridge scholar, Pembroke college, whose portrait appears in the frontispiece.

James Butler (17) 1710, April 6, m. Abigail Eustiss, by Rev. Ebenezer Pemberton, pastor of the Old South (1672 1717). He d. 1715. She d. 1713. &c.)5,

Their children were :

22. Abigail, b. 1710-11, Jan. 26, m. Jacob Hitchcock, July 3, 1738.

23. Elizabeth[2], b. 1711 12, March 3, m. Samuel Cravath, April 19, 1733.

24. James[3], b. 1713, Dec. 4, m. Elizabeth Davie.

James Butler's (17) second wife was Mary Bowditch of Salem, dau. of William and Mary (Gardner) Bowditch.

Their only child was carried to Salem by its widowed mother, about 1715.

Elizabeth Butler (23) with her husband Cravath, m. in 1733, by Rev. Thos. Foxcroft, pastor of First church 1716 69 (Gen. Reg. xlii, p. 55), soon removed to Middletown (Conn.) and d. there. A tomb in that place is inscribed : " Here lies the body of Mrs. Elizabeth Cravath who died March 30, 1740," aged 28 years." Her husband was son of Ezekiel and Elizabeth Hooks C., who were published at Salisbury, Mass., May 28, 1698 and were m. in Boston, June 14, 1698.

Abigail Eustiss wife of James Butler (17) was b. 1690, Feb. Her parents were John (b. 1 65 J, Dec. 8) and Elizabeth Eustiss. The parents of this John, were William and Sarah. She d. 1713, Dec. 15, eleven days after the birth of her son James (24).

James Butler (17) b. 1688, Aug. 21. He d. 1715, Oct. m. Abigail Eustiss, 1710. April 6, and also m. Mary Bowditch.

His estate. At the request of his widow and

children who were minors, William Bowditch of
Salem, mariner [father of Mr. Butler's second
wife] and John Eustiss of Boston, housewright
[father of Mr. Butler's first wife] were appointed
administrators of the estate of James Butler of
Boston, rope-maker, deceased. They returned into
the Probate Court an inventory of said estate,
taken Oct. 27, 1715, by Samuel Barrett and Joseph
Billings.

The house and land of James Butler adjoined
those of Thomas Jackson a distiller who had married Mr. Butler's sister (15) in 1706, and who probably brought up his three orphan children.

Extracts from the Butler Inventory, 1715:

House lot £160, Negro woman Dinah £30, silver
ware £20, 18s., 2d., one-sixth of Sloop *Mary* £16,
1 bay mare, 1 red cow, 1 heifer and calf £17,
pewter and brass ware £16, 6s., table linen £13,
7s., 4 suits clothes and riding coat £17, 4s., sheets
and pillow biers £28, clock and two tables £12, 16s.,
chairs, looking-glass and table £13, 18s., curtains,
bedstead, quilt and blankets £17, green curtains,
bed, bolster and pillows £26, other items amount-
in all to £510, 10s., 10d.

About two years afterwards in 1717, these administrators returned an additional account of
moneys which had come into their hands, viz :
From Benjamin Gallup† on bonds,   £101 11 10
From Capt. John Ballantine,   .   .   £ 34 17 6

---

† Perhaps a relative of Benjamin (4) Butler's wife.

From James Oliver,   .   £ 23 8 4
From Joseph Gardner,*   .   £ 37 8 10
From N. Tead, ... £ 14 14 6
From James & John Barton and
     Eliza Simpkins,   .   £214 0 0
From Sundry others,   .   £351 3 6
                                    £777 4 6

Among the charges made by the administrators for moneys paid out by them were the following :

Funeral charges £12, 14s, widow's mourning £5, 3s., 10d., nursing the widow £1, 5s., calash hire and expenses of carrying the widow to Salem £1, 6s., 6d , wages of Hannah Simpson for keeping house £18, 19s. Thomas Jackson (20) for opening a drain 12s., debts £43, 19s. 11¾d, charges in arresting James Barton £3, 6s.

John Eustiss died in 1723, leaving £1049, 3s. 6d, and William Bowditch died 1728 9, Feb. 7. They left Butler's estate more than fourteen years after his death still unsettled, and Joseph and Ebenezer, sons of Bowditch, were appointed to complete the settlement. No record of their proceedings has thus far come to light. The three children were probably brought up by their aunt Jackson.

FIFTH GENERATION AND THEIR CHILDREN.

James Butler (24) b. 1713, m. 1739, May 17, Elizabeth Davie. His death was ———. her death was in Feb. 1740, at the birth of her only child.

---

* Perhaps a kinsman of Butler's (17) second wife.

25. Their child was James[4] b. 1739–40, Feb. 15.
The second wife of James (24) m. 1744, Nov. 29,
was Sarah Wakefield.

26. Their only child, Sarah d. unmarried, and
her parents did not long live together.

James Butler (24) b. 1713, was by occupation a
goldsmith. Thanks perhaps to his marriage into
the Davie family, and yet more to whole-souled
social qualities, he was a favorite among British
officers in Boston. It is said that they found a welcome rendevous in a back room of his shop. As
was natural, he became politically a tory, socially a
high-liver, and financially a bankrupt. His wife's
death within a year after marriage cut him loose
from social ties. Their only child, James, brought
up from infancy away from him, was already the
head of a family when the Revolution drew nigh,
and was urged by his father to seek a refuge in the
British Provinces. He is said to have been saved
from such a flight by the influence of his own wife
Mary Sigourney, who had a great dread of any
pioneering analogous to that of her Huguenot
grandmother in Oxford, a century before (801).
James (24) the father, however, made his way to
Halifax but came back poorer than he went, and
was afterwards largely supported by his son.
Among that son's papers there are the following
receipts.

"Received of James Butler, Jun., nine pounds
twelve shillings for boarding your father from Sept.
7th, 1768, to July 5, 1769.

By me, Solomon Holman.

Received of James Butler £7, 10s., 8d., L. M.
[Lawful Money] in full for boarding his Father from
July 5, 1769, to April 5th, 1770, thirty-nine weeks
at 4s. a week.

SOLOMON HOLMAN.

These receipts were for money paid in Boston,
but Mr. Holman's home was in Sutton,—and he
was a kinsman of the Butlers. James Butler was
probably an invalid and was placed in the country
for his health. He used to come into Boston on
horseback, leaving his horse at the south end, and
walking to his son's home which was at the north
end. His grandson, James Davie (28) says, "when I
was still a small boy I was sent one morning with
my grandfather who was leaving us, to carry his
bundle for him as he went to his horse. On the
way he sat down to rest on the steps of the Stone
Chapel. I was surprised that he was so feeble."

Sabine in his work on American Loyalists (p. 187.)
remarks. "James Butler in 1776, embarked at
Boston for Halifax with the British Army." No
doubt he had been in the city during its siege.
Whether he ever returned again to his native State
seems to me doubtful. There is a tradition of boys
in Sutton hooting at him as a tory. But such
maltreatment may have befallen him as well before
the Revolution as after.

DAVIE FAMILY.

Regarding the lineage of *Elizabeth Davie* with
whom the name Davie came into the Butler family
(24) I have gathered the following particulars.

1 D. John Davie, of Creedy, m. Juliann Strode, of Neunham, Kent. In 1662, one of their children, Humphrey, emigrated to Connecticut. His second wife was Sarah Gibbons Richards, of Hartford.

2 D. His son, John, graduated at Harvard, in 1681, and in 1707, became a baronet. (See New London, Caulkins.)

3 D. Humphrey, who was brother of the baronet, and b. 1673, in Hartford.

4 D. ——, m. 1714, April 22, ~~Hannah~~ [or Margaret?] Gedney.

5 D. Their daughter Elizabeth, b. 1715-16, m. 1739, May 17, James Butler (24).

H. F. Waters (p. 27.) says that in 1730, Bartholomew Gedney, of Boston, m. 1731, Oct. 28, Sarah Johnson, was appointed guardian of Elizabeth Davie, then about fourteen years of age.

6 D. William Gedney, of Salem, b. 1668, d. 1730, m. 1690, Hannah Gardner.

7 D. Among their children was ~~Hannah~~ [or Margaret], b. 1694, June 8, who m. Humphrey Davie (3 D).

SIXTH GENERATION AND THEIR CHILDREN.

James Butler, (2.) b. 1740, m. 1763, May 10, Mary Sigourney, b. 1741, Mar. 23, (822). He d. 1827, Dec. 20, Oxford. She d. 1823, April. 14, Oxford.

Their children were :

27. Mary[3], b. 1764, Mar. 4, Sun. 4 A. M., Boston.
28. James Davie[1], b. 1765, Oct. 5, Sat. 11 A. M, Boston.

29. Anthony¹. b. 1767, Oct. 8, Thurs. 2 P. M.,
Boston.
30. Elizabeth². b. 1770, Feb. 9, Fri. 10 P. M.,
Boston.
31. Hannah¹, b. 1771, Dec. 5, Thurs. P. M.,
Boston.
32. John¹, b. 1773, July 4, Sun. 7 A. M., Boston.
33. Peter¹, b. 1774, Dec. 16, Fri. 11 P. M., Kennebec.
34. Sarah¹, b. 1776, Sep. 29, Sun. 11 A. M., Kennebec.
35. Celia¹, b. 1779, Apr. 25, Sun. A. M., Boston.
Hannah Butler (31) d. Oxford, 1792, Feb. 6.

JAMES BUTLER.

James Butler (25). For some reason it was
desired to have proof of his baptism, and so the
following certificate was procured many years after.
It is still in my hands.

BOSTON, 10 Feb'y, 1795.
"This may certify that James Butler was baptized
on the 17th day of Feb'y 1740, by the Rev'd Mr.
Gray, one of the Pastors of the New Brick church.
Attest,   JOHN LATHROP,
                               Pastor."

His mother dying at his birth, his infancy was
cared for by his aunt Tileston five miles out of town.
At fourteen he was bound as an apprentice to his
uncle Jackson (19), a hatter and also a distiller. At
twenty-three he married and was already in business

for himself, as appears by a MS. book of receipts still preserved. One of these papers shows that he was already (1763) sending hats to the West Indies. From others it appears that he then paid rent on three buildings at £12, £10, £8, 10s., per annum.

One of these rents I suppose was for his dwelling, another for his shop, and the third for his father.

He redeemed various articles of his mother's dress which his father had pawned, and that have since been handed down as heir-looms. Besides high-heeled shoes, and a silver rattle with coral and bells, one of these is a brocade with a skirt of seven breadths,—the bodice long and to be worn with a satin stomacher, sleeves short at elbows with flowing ruffles. Out of another of these dresses, a watered silver silk, we have cut a christening blanket, or what Shakespeare calls a *bearing-cloth*. My children were all baptized in it.

In 1774, the Port Bill, dating from March 29, destroyed the business of Boston. Mr. B. (25), was then the father of six children. He owned the house in which he lived. It was brick, of two stories, in Prince street, opposite Snow Hill street, and near Thatcher, in going east from Salem street. In 1829, I saw it still in fair condition, and raised one story higher.

Unable to live longer in Boston Mr. B., with some friends chartered a schooner, secretly put on board their families and household stuff, ran the blockade in a fog, and fled to the Kennebec River in August, 1774. Starting on Sunday night the 6th, they arrived at Arrowsic Island on Thursday. This island, seven miles below Bath, is opposite Phippsburg and near a rocky and bushy bluff called Squirrel Point. In 1850, the little white house in which my grandfather here found shelter at an annual rent of £4, was still standing, and on the hill-top above was the two story dwelling of his landlord William Butler. The white house was near the water, and the boys. James in his tenth year, and Anthony but little younger learned to manage a boat before they had ever mounted a horse. They could also soon fish and hunt. Thus they helped supply the family with food.

About 1763, Daniel Sigourney (827) had brought from Canada a quantity of French arms, — spoils of war. One fowling-piece given to his son Andrew (b. 1738) had been given by him to his cousin James Butler and was taken to the Kennebec. His oldest son Davie, was early a marksman with this weapon. One of his first successes was shooting a wild goose, which however fell into water so deep that he at first despaired of securing his prize. But he called on his brother Anthony for help. Neither boy could swim. The younger waded in as far as he dared, and the older, holding by his hand, ventured in further, so that he was at last able to clutch the bird's wing. This feathered spoil was viewed by the mother with a trembling joy. She trembled at the risk her little ones had run, and yet she rejoiced that she could serve up to her household a more appetizing dainty than had been seen on her table for weeks. Besides, the boys ere long became swimmers so that her fears of drowning were less. In Boston her anxiety had been that they would be carried off by press-gangs to serve as cabin boys on British ships.

The landlord of Mr. Butler had built in the woods a house of hiding where he promised my grandmother to shelter her and her brood, if any British cruiser should lay waste the settlement. A hostile vessel did indeed once come up the river, but James Butler, going on board with other citizens, made such a truce that no violence was done.

About a year after the exiles arrived, that is Sept. 21, 1775, Arnold's corps passed the island on their wilderness march to Quebec. Not many weeks after, not a few of them, disabled on the way, came down from above, haggard and halting, barefoot and half naked.

Raccoon, musquash and beaver being at hand, Mr. Butler was able to do much work in hat-making.

In October, 1778, his family returned to Boston, but he, with his oldest son, James, remained a month longer. He paid rent up to November 20th. He made a voyage from Boston to Penobscot, carrying coffee and other goods which he hoped to exchange for furs. His arrival there was too early, for the hunters had not yet come in from their hunting-grounds. Leaving his stock in charge of one Carey, he returned to Boston and arrived there on the very day that the British seized

Penobscot, June 17, 1779. A narrow escape from capture.

Business not reviving in Boston, he bought a farm in Oxford, 50 acres for $1,000.00 in continental bills which had not yet greatly depreciated. His purchase was of his wife's cousin Abraham Waters, who lived in Sutton.

Here he resided till his death, Dec. 20, 1827. From October 1779, he was innkeeper, hatter, farmer and merchant. His establishment is thus described in Stockwell's Oxford (p. 178): "Butler's Tavern in the territorial center of Oxford was built, it is believed, before 1778. It stands on the west side of the old common, and to-day (1879) it is covered by the same shaved clapboards held by the same hand-wrought nails that were attached to it at the time of its erection. On the turn-pike between Worcester and Norwich it was in its day a noted resort and stage-station. It was said that the rum sold at this place in a day would float one of his majesty's ships. In 1799, the officers of the so-called Adams' army of four regiments had their head-quarters at this tavern.

The bar-room is unchanged, but the bar is not there. In this room was the first store in Oxford, kept by Andrew Sigourney (826) and James Butler (25). A partition was erected in one corner enclosing a space of about six feet by four. In this enclosure were kept and sold buttons, shoe and knee buckles and tobacco: molasses and cod-fish were stored in the cellar."

In 1780, Mr. B., made a journey eastward overland, stole into the British post at Penobscot, and
bought the beaver he needed for hat-making.
During all 'his month within the enemy's lines he
was in danger of being sent to Halifax as a prisoner
or rather as a spy. Once after going up to bed he
overheard, as he thought, his landlady betray him to
custom officers who came to her for entertainment.
All night in suspense, he was often on the point of
leaping down from his chamber window and seeking
to escape. But at dawn his night fears vanished,
when the lady of the house assured him she had
not spoken of him at all.

In 1786, he was town treasurer; in 1794–1795
and 1809 he represented the town in the Legis
lature. In 1806, he sold off his stock of goods
to his son Peter,—and though he lived more than
twenty years longer, he engaged in no active business. He was visiting his son James in Rutland,
Vt., in 1814, when news came of the naval victory
at Plattsburg on Sept. 14th. Though seventy-four
years old, he is described as dancing at the bonfires,
throwing up his hat and huzzaing like a boy at the
cannon-firing. His religious preferences were
Sandemanian.

Mary Sigourney, mother of (27) et seqq., learned
French from her grandmother, mother of (807)
et seqq. She retained something of it to the end
of her life. In 1815, she was interviewed at her
home in Oxford, by Dr. Holmes, father of Oliver
Wendell. Her family traditions, thus gathered,

4

were published in the Massachusetts Historical
collections. (3d Series, Vol. II. p. 79.)

Mary Butler (27) was called odd from her childhood and insane onward from middle life. A great
fire in Boston gave her a shock from which she
never recovered. Between 1790 and 1800 she came
to live with her brother James in Rutland, keeping
house for him and perhaps assisting in his store.
Soon after 1820 she began to live entirely alone,
south of the village in the first house on the left
after crossing Moon's Brook. From early boyhood
I used more than once a week to carry her a
basket of milk, butter, meat, or other necessaries.
Her oddities in dress, conversation and behavior
made her cottage a daily resort of the curious. In
1839, Sept. 25, she was brought to my father's
house, and continued there till her death at the age
of 83, in 1847, Dec. 22d.

Being very plain looking, she used to say that
she had been a handsome child, but was in fact not
herself, but a changling, changed in the cradle by
fairies for one of their homely brats.

JAMES DAVIE BUTLER, I.

James Davie Butler (28) b. Boston 1765, d. Rutland, Vt., 1842. His schooling in childhood seems
to have been under Master Tileston at the North
writing school (810). Some incidents of his life
between the ages of nine and thirteen, during the
family flight to Maine, have been already men

tioned. Had his father made his country home, as
was at one time his purpose, in Leicester, the
Academy, founded there in 1784, would surely have
led him to a college education, for books and the
study of them were his life-long passion.

He learned grammar from one Shumway, while
the other children were the scholars of a Dr.
Walker, who, for fear of betraying his own ignorance, would never let them parse. He had begun
teaching in his father's district in the winter of
1786-7, but when volunteers were called for in the
Shay's rebellion, he enlisted in the government
service.

In June 1787, he visited with his kinsman Col.
Holman, Rutland, Vt., which though settled as
early as 1770, had been largely deserted during the
Revolution, but was now reviving. In August of
the same year he came there again with his father,
and decided to make Rutland his home, though he
was strongly tempted to stop with Bellows near
Walpole, fifty miles nearer his Massachusetts
cradle. His first journeys to and fro were on
horseback with a bag of silver on the pommel of
the saddle, but he soon began to drive down a pair
of horses, carrying fur and ginseng and to return
with a load of merchandise.

He at once began hat-making, and in 1790 was
joined by his brother Anthony to whom he gave
up that business in 1792, and became a merchant,
continuing one for fifty years. For a long time he
was successful. In 1816, when the United States

tax was collected (H. Clay by Schurz, I. p. 129), his
name, assessed at $9,667, headed the list of Rutland
tax-payers. In after years he met with reverses :
in 1836 he ceased to buy goods, but kept open his
store and was selling off his old stock for six years
longer. He had several tenant farms and much
wild land, all which, being sold before the railroad era, proved unprofitable.

He was for many years town treasurer, or select-
man, and in 1813 and 1815 town representative in
the Vermont Legislature. In early life he was
sceptically inclined from French principles then in
the air, but about the year 1813 he came to a hearty
belief in the Bible, the whole Bible and nothing but
the Bible, as man's rule of faith and practice. In
that year 1813, he united with the Congregational
church and died thirty years after in its commu-
nion. His death June 3, 1842, occurred when I
was in New York on my way to travel abroad, but
I hurried to Rutland and attended his funeral.

His first marriage was in 1802, Aug. 22, to
Rachel Maynard, a widow with two daughters.

Rachel Maynard, b. *Harris* (511), had as her first
husband Trowbridge Maynard, son of James and
Zeruiah (Johnson) Maynard of Westborough, Mass.,
where he was b. in 1767, July 30, d. Rutland 1801,
Aug. 14.

Their children were,

Laura, b. 1796, Feb. 7, d. 1815, July 13.

Eliza, b. 1801, Oct. 8, d. 1825, April 29. Both
were buried in the graveyard north of village.

RESIDENCE OF JAMES DAVIE BUTLER, RUTLAND, VT.

The children of James Davie Butler (28) (he d. 1842. June 3) and Rachel (Harris) Maynard (511) (she d. 1822, Feb. 10.) were :

36. 1. Twin daughters, b. 1803, March 19, d. in infancy.

37. 2. Mary Sigourney, b. 1804, Sept. 11, d. 1833, Aug. 17. No. 74.

38. 3 Sophia Gedney, 1807, Jan. 16, d. 1826, Jan. 14.

39. 4 Chloe Harris, 1810, March 22.

40. 5 James Davie^2, 1814, Jan. 6, d. in infancy.

41. 6 James Davie^3, 1815, March 15.

All these children were born at Rutland in the house their father had built about the year 1800. It was of two stories and brick. Its front 55 and its depth 36 feet. with an annex in the middle of the rear running back as much farther. It faces the west, standing on *Main* street, and originally had battlements at each end, but no end window at all. Thanks to this lack, it escaped destruction in 1843 when a wooden house on the south, separated only by a driveway, burned and fell down against the windowless wall. The walls were a foot thick and when I sold the house in 1867, were pronounced by masons as good as ever. A cordon, or band of white marble, girdles the house between the stories. In 1887, July 19, this house was bid off at auction for $6,350. (See engraving.)

The south half of this edifice was the store of Mr.
Butler for more than forty years. The brass
knocker on the front door was the American
eagle with arrows in one claw and an olive
branch in the other, the shield on its breast inscribed. *J. D. Butler.* Four fire-places were bor-
dered with tiles, each painted with one of Æsop's
fables. The high wall-clock, with "Nichols God-
dard No. 11." on the face, stood sometimes in the
hall, and sometimes in the dining-room annex.

This antique relic as well as the knocker above
mentioned, I transported in 1866 to Madison, Wis.,
where it has kept good time ever since. It must
date from the first years in the nineteenth century
and may be still older.

The second wife of James D. Butler (28) m. 1827.
March 15 was own cousin of the first, namely,
Miss Lois Harris (552), who d. Rutland, Vt., 1866,
Aug. 5.

Anthony Butler (29) b. 1767, he d. 1847. March
13. m. Jerusha Hill, b. Oxford, Mass., 1773. she d.
in Rutland, Vt. 1795, Sept. 20.

Their children were :

42.   Mary[2], m. Abram Owen, No. 88.

43.   Hannah[3], m. Sterns De Witt.

44.   James D.[4], b. 1795, July 25.

His second wife was Deborah Hill, a sister of his
first. She d. 1820.

Their children were :

45.   1 Lucinda, d. early.

46.   2 Peter H., b. 1801.

47. 3 Jerusha, m. Sylvester Lyon.
48. 4 Sarah[2], m. Benjamin F. Williams.
49. 7 Arpasia, b. 1811.
50. 8 Lucretia[1], b. 1811, m. John Ogle, living
    in 1887.

51. Twins.
    { 5 Elizabeth[4], b. 1806, March 13, m.
                Kennedy Brooks.
    { 6 Celia.

52. 9 Julia Hill, b. 1813, m. Thomas Hutchin-
    son, M. D. and for second husband, A. B.
    Young, Somerville, Butler Co.
53. 10 John[2], d. 1815, March 15, in Vt.

His third wife was Eunice Riley, m. 1822.

Anthony Butler (29) b. 1767; in 1786 volunteered
at the first call for troops to put down the Shay
rebellion. Through exposure in this service he
became hard of hearing, and continued so through
life. After some years in Rutland, Vt., he settled
in 1796 on a farm of a hundred acres in the adjoining town of Pittsford. About twenty years afterward in 1817, he sold his farm to Samuel Fairfield
and emigrated to Ohio. Fixing his residence in
Oxford, Butler Co., he continued there till his death
in 1847, March 13.

After resolving on removal he was detained for
some time that his family might take a course of
small pox, by inoculation. He left his Vermont
home on the last day of September. His wife
drove one of three wagons, and his son Peter
another. A series of way-side letters to his brother
James in Rutland, Vt., I have published. Three of

them were mailed at Montgomery, Orange
Co., N. Y., Oct. 10. Loudon, Franklin Co., Pa.,
Oct. 23, and Pittsburgh, Nov. 12. In the last
mentioned place he had purchased for $60 an ark
with a deck, fire-place and other conveniences,
large enough to transport his wagons, five horses,
and all the havings of a family he had fallen in
with from Gardner in Maine. He was still in
doubt whether to stop in Athens, or go on to Cincinnati. It was fifty-eight days after starting
from Vermont before he reached Cincinnati.

In crossing Laurel Ridge, three miles up and
four miles down, he found no house, and camped
on the summit. In his own words : " Cutting poles
and crotches he covered them with the painted
wagon canvass, and built a fire against a log,
daughters dismayed, night rainy, big dog on the
watch till morning."

He was told, just before he launched on the Ohio,
that the week before, men, women and children
were seen on the deck of a boat calling for help, but
that none could be rendered. He was a Mason, and
thus writes: " In the neighborhood of Pittsburgh I
got acquainted with John Grove, the man at whose
house I put up. I showed him the certificate which
Captain Lord had handed me from the Royal Arch
Chapter. He went into the city and on his return
told me, that if I was in distress there was $300,
in Pittsburgh, and quarters for me and my family
at some of the best houses. I told him that I
thanked him and them, but —— we shoved off

our ark, minded to lie by at night, and to inquire on the way which side of islands to steer. Just then Grove cried out to us that a stranger who said he was a seaman would pilot us down, if we would give him a passage. Near the close of November the ark arrived in Cincinnati."

Elizabeth Butler (30) m. 1793, Sept. 1, Jeremiah Kingsbury. . She d. 1830, Aug. 28. He d. 1842, Feb. 10, b. 1763, Aug. 21.

Their children were:

54 Davie Butler b. 1795, June 19, d. 1882.

55. Hannah, b. 1797, Feb. 9, d. 1869, Dec. 15.

56. Laura, b. 1807, Feb 21.

Sarah Butler (34) sister of Elizabeth was the second wife of Jeremiah Kingsbury, m. ——

John Butler (32) b. 1773, m. Sarah Fisk, b. Oxford. · He d. 1824, Sept. 25, Oxford. She d. in Dedham.

Their children were :

57. Celia², b. 1796, Nov. 22, Rutland, Vt.

58. Susan, b. ——

59. Mary¹, b. Spencer, Mass.

John Butler (32) followed his brother James from Oxford to Rutland, Vt., worked as a hatter there for some years onward from 1794. One of the first years in the new century he opened a store in Spencer, Mass, In 1805 he failed and left the country. On Nov. 17th of that year, a letter from him to his brother James who had been security and paid money for him, was dated, Danbury (Conn).

In Jeffersonville (Ind.) he was made keeper of the hotel of Maj. Wm. Christy, but in Feb. 1806, he passed on to St. Louis. There on the 23d of the next Sept., he saw the arrival of Lewis and Clark returning from the Pacific. In their party he recognized in Robert Frazer one of his old Rutland debtors, and secured payment. He was employed in the lead mines of Moses Austin, near St. Genevieve, and was in a house thrown down by the earthquake of 1811. Once while creeping among some bushes to shoot a deer, a twig just before his face was cut off by the bullet of some one lurking to shoot him. All went ill with him. A trunk of valuables dispatched to him by friends in Oxford and Rutland, via New Orleans, was lost by the way. Turning his earnings into lead he started to carry it to market, but his boat striking a snag, he was well nigh drowned in the Mississippi. He joined a trading company that adventured up the Arkansas, but the enterprise proved a failure.

During the war of 1812 he served in the regular army. The Army Register (p. 107) sets him down, second lieutenant, Aug. 14, 1813, and on March 17, 1814, first lieutenant, in the twenty-fourth infantry. His captain was Robert Desha, and his colonel, E. P. Gaines.

He was stationed at Fort Osage, Jackson Co., Missouri, founded 1808, 300 miles up the river and near the present site of Kansas City. It is described by Brackenbridge in 1811. (Louisaina. p. 217.) Penned in by Indians, his command had no rations but potatoes, while buffaloes were roving before their eyes. They were at last obliged to burn the Fort and escape down the river in boats. Among his other stations were St. Charles, Bellefontaine and Fort Clark. In January 1814, he was acting Adjutant at Newport, Ky., keeping guard over 400 British prisoners. He writes from Detroit, May 14, 1814; that he had marched thither from Newport across the State of Ohio, that 400 regulars were in Detroit, and that 400 militia had just pushed on to establish a post ninety miles above. His force reaching St. Joseph, July 20, destroyed it, and also British stores at St. Mary's, arriving at Mackinaw, July 26. On Aug. 4, 900 Americans landed, were attacked by Indians in thick bushes, and fought there forty minutes, losing 87 killed or wounded : they returned to their boats. In Lieut. Butler's company the Captain. Desha, was shot through the thigh, the third Lieut. Jackson, and six privates were killed, Butler's own sword-belt was cut by a bullet. Gen. Cullum's account of the action is as follows,: (p. 200), "Aug. 4. Our land force attempted an attack from a height in the rear of the Fort, which resulted in a sharp conflict chiefly with Indians in a thick wood, and the retreat of our troops."

John Butler was not a large man, but of uncommon strength and agility. In youth he was a celebrated wrestler.

Peter Butler (33) b. 1774. He d. 1856. Dec. 30,
m. Mehitabel Corbin. She d. 1336, Dec. 2, of
lung fever.

Their children were :

60. James[1], b. 1802.
61. Samuel[2], b. 1804, Jan. 10.
62. Lucy, b. 1805, Dec. 30.
63. Mary S.[2], b. 1808, April 5.
64. Eliza, b. 1810, Aug. 28.
65. Sarah[4], b. 1815, Sept. 13.
66. Hannah[4], b. 1817, Sept. 30.
67. Peter[2], b. 1820, Jan. 6.
68. Charlotte, b. 1824, Aug. 18.

Celia Butler (35) b. 1779, m. Archibald Campbell[2*]. He was b. 1776, d. 1818, Oct, 5. She d
1851, May 20, in Boston.

————

* The earliest ancestor I can trace of this Archibald[2] was Rev.
John Campbell, pastor of the church in Oxford from 1721, March 1,
to 1761, May 21, the date of his death. Born in the north of Scotland about 1690, of University education, according to tradition he
was a political refugee about 1717, and was visited as an old friend
by Lord Loudon (b. 1705], in July 1756. The place of their parting
on a bridge between the parsonage and Oxford plain was early
pointed out to me by my father, to the north east of the village.
—Wolcott *Memorial*, p. 200.

John Campbell above mentioned m. Esther Fairchild.

Their children were: Mary, b. 1723, m. Jacob Town. John, b.
1724, Isabella b. 1726, m. Josiah Wolcott, whose dau. Eliza m.
Andrew Sigourney (826), Duncan b. 1727. Elizabeth b. 1730, Alexander b. 1732, William b. 1734, Archibald[1], b. 1736.

Duncan Campbell m. Elizabeth Stearns, b. 1736' d. 1821.

Their children were Thomas, Samuel, John, Alexander, Lucretia
m. John Walker, Archibald[2], m. Celia Butler. (35)'

PETER BUTLER.

Their children were :

69. Archibald[4]. b. 1804.

70. Benjamin Franklin, b. 1806, July 6.

71. James Butler, b. 1808, Oct. 27.

72 Mary Butler, b, 1812, May 26.

73. Celia Elizabeth, b. 1817, Aug. 18.

Celia Butler (35) seems to have owed her christian name to her aunt Celia Loring Sigourney (855).

Mary B. Campbell (72) was living in Columbia, S. C., when that city was captured by Gen. Sherman in 1865. Her house had been selected by an Aide of Gen. Rusk, of Wisconsin, for that officer's head-quarters. Thanks to this circumstance it escaped the plunder and conflagration which befell so many.

EIGHTH GENERATION AND THEIR CHILDREN.

Mary Sigourney Butler (37) m. Horace Green. She d. 1833, Aug. 17, Rutland, Vt. He d. 1866, Nov. 29 at Sing Sing.

74. Their only child was Ann Sophia, b. 1832, April 27 in Rutland, Vt., m. at Sing Sing, N. Y., 1876, June 1, S. B. Loveland, of Pittsford, Vt.

Mary S. Butler (37) was a pupil in Troy at the school of Madam Emma Willard in 1822-3. She was m. in 1829, Oct. 20th, by Rev. Willard Child, at her father's house.

Horace Green (74) b. Chittenden, Vt. 1802, Dec. 24, was a physician in Rutland, Vt., and afterwards in the city of New York. In bronchial diseases, which he soon made a specialty, his success was great, bring-

ing him much of fame and fortune. His second
wife was Harriet Douglas, whose brother, John H.
Douglas, trained up by Dr. Green, acquired a con-
tinental reputation as the chief medical attendant
of General Grant during his last illness.

Mary Sigourney Butler (37) b. 1804, m. Horace
Green in 1829, Oct. 20, and died four years after-
wards, in 1833, Aug. 17. Their only child, Ann
Sophia. b. in Rutland in 1832, April 27, m. S. B.
Loveland of Pittsford, Vt., at Sing Sing, N. Y. in
1876, June 1.

Mary Sigourney's (37) constitution was broken by
a fever in childhood. Yet she was a pupil in Mrs.
Willard's school in Troy, N. Y. in 1823-4. She had
instruction in music, dancing, French and drawing.
In the last she excelled. Many specimens of her
painting were treasured by her friends for a genera
tion after her death.

Chloe H. Butler (39) b. 1810, m. 1831. Jan. 27,
John Smith Cleveland, in Salem, N. Y. He d. 1863,
Aug. 27, Burton, O.

Their children were :

75. Mary Elizabeth, born Jan. 8, 1832, Whitehall,
    N. Y.

76. James Butler, b. Feb. 14, 1834, Pawlet, Vt.

77. Ann Butler, b. Oct. 31, 1836, Akron, O.

78. Jane Harris, b. Oct. 30, 1839, Granger, O.

79. Laura Pease, b. Aug. 1, 1842, Brecksville, O.

80. Ellen Douglas, born March 16, 1845, Hunts-
    burg, O.

81. John Smith, b. Sept. 30, 1847, Burton, O.

Ellen Cleveland (80) d. early and unmarried.

John S. Cleveland (81) was killed by a rocket in Chardon, O., July 4, 1884, leaving no children.

Mary E. Cleveland (75) married ―――― Johnson. Their only child was a daughter, Jane.

James B. Cleveland (76), as Lieutenant in the 41st Ohio Regiment, was in battles at Shiloh, Stone River, and elsewhere. After the war he was long a Treasury clerk at Washington.

James D. Butler[3] (41) b. 1815, m. 1845, April 21, Anna Bates, at the Cong. church in Dudley, Mass., by Rev. Dr. Joshua Bates, the bride's father.

Their children were :

82. James Davie[5], born 1846, June 25, 6 P. M. Norwich, Vt.

83. William Bates, b. 1848, Feb. 3, 11 P. M. Wells River, Vt.

84. Mary Bates, b. 1850, January 6, 11 A. M. Wells River, Vt.

85. Henry Sigourney, b. 1854, Nov. 16, 10 P. M. in sixth street, Cincinnati, O.

86. Anna Bates, b. 1860, July 2, 1 A. M. Madison, Wis.

87. Agnes Campbell, born 1863, Dec. 20, 3 A. M. Madison, Wisconsin.

James Davie Butler (82) m. 1880, April 22, Sarah Adamson in Marshalltown, Iowa. She was born in Boonboro', Boon Co. Iowa, 1856, Feb. 22, d. Chicago, 1887, Oct. 6.

Wm. B. Butler (83) died of cholera in Cincinnati, 1854. Aug. 1.

Mary B. Butler (84) died in South Danvers (now Peabody) 1851, Sept. 28.

J. D. Butler[5] (82), while under military age, was a drummer in Company D, 40th Wisconsin Infantry. He enlisted again as a private in Company H, 49th Wisconsin Infantry.

James Davie Butler[2] (41) b. Rutland, Vt., 1815, March 15, was considered a consumptive child, and long before he was eight years old was treated with blood-letting as a prophylactic. In 1829, Oct. 29, he started for Boston, and there served as lowest boy for eight months, in the hardware store of his cousin, James Butler, (60) at Nos. 9 and 13 Dock square. The next summer, returning home to Rutland, he soon began studying Latin in the select school of a Baptist minister, Rev. Hadley Proctor. In 1831, April 27, he left home to prepare for college at the Wesleyan Seminary in Wilbraham, Mass. He remained there till May 10th of the next year. The next four years he was in Middlebury College, and was graduated there in 1836. His oration, on "The Poetical Merit of the Iliad," appeared in the Quarterly Register, Feb. 1837. Leaving Rutland on the 19th of the next September, he was a year in the Theological School of Yale College. For five terms onward, till December, 1838, he was a tutor at Middlebury College, and, on the death of Prof. Turner, acting professor for nearly a year. In 1862 the degree of LL.D. was conferred on him by this college.

He arrived in Andover at the close of November, 1838, and graduated at the seminary there in 1840. His oration was on "Chrysostom as a Preacher." Having been elected an Abbott resident, he continued to reside at the seminary as a post-graduate —board, apartments, etc. being furnished for him from the Abbott fund.

In 1842, June 23rd, he sailed from New York, with Prof. Edwards A. Park, in the Hamburg packet Howard. Their first travels were from Hamburg to the Hartz and Frankfort, and then, during the vintage season, in a pedestrian tour between Cologne and Mannheim. From Heidelberg they proceeded to Jena, halting at Hanau, Fulda, Erfurt, Gotha and Weimar. They then separated, in order to be forced to speak German altogether.

Mr. Butler studied for some months at the universities of Jena, Halle and Berlin, then via. Dresden, Prague, Vienna and Venice, journeyed to Rome and Naples. Returning by way of Florence, Genoa and Milan, he spent the summer of 1843 in Alpine wanderings. then stopped for some time in Paris, London and their environs. After visits to Scotland and Ireland he reached America in the last month of 1843.

The same winter he began to deliver European lectures, then a rarity, and while abroad had corresponded for the New York *Observer*. He was engaged as a supply of Congregational pulpits, in West Newbury, Mass.. and Burlington, Vermont—

5

six months in each. For two years onward from
September, 1845, he was professor, or acting President, of the University at Norwich, Vt. During
these years he delivered many lectures and supplied
pulpits. While preaching at Burlington he was
married at Dudley, Mass., to Miss Anna Bates (334),
April 21, 1845. In 1847, Oct. 14, he was settled as
pastor of the church in Wells River, Vt. In 1851,
Feb. 26, after a few months as professor and pulpit-
supply in Norwich, he was installed pastor of the
Congregational church in South Danvers, Mass.
(now Peabody), and was dismissed from the same
Aug. 4, 1852. His farewell discourse here—and a
sermon at the burial of an officer killed at the
storming of Chepultepec—were published. On Nov.
18th of the same year, 1852, he became pastor of the
First Congregational church in Cincinnati, Ohio.
On leaving this pulpit, having served as professor
of Greek in Wabash College, Crawfordsville, Ind.,
from January, 1855, to the close of the college year
in 1858, he accepted a similar position in the University of Wisconsin. He taught there nine years,
till the close of the college year of 1867. . His
"Defence of Classical Studies," or "How a Dead
Language Makes a Live Man," delivered as his
inaugural in 1858 in the Senate chamber at Madison,
was repeated at New Bedford before the American
Institute of Instruction, in Detroit before the National Educational Association, at various college
commencements, and in more than fifty other
places.

In 1867, August 7, he landed in Liverpool, and traveled widely for more than a year. Among his halting-places were London, Copenhagen, St. Petersburg, Moscow, Berlin, Cologne, Paris, Madrid, Toledo, Cordova, Seville, Cadiz, Gibraltar, Malaga, Granada, Saragossa, Barcelona, Marseilles, Rome, Naples, Messina, Alexandria, Cairo, the first cataract, Suez, Port Said, Joppa, Jerusalem, Hebron, Nazareth, Hasbeiyah, Damascus, Balbec, Beyroot, Mersina, Rhodes, Smyrna, Constantinople, Athens, Corinth, Delphi, Bologna, Florence, Venice, Munich, Nuremberg, a dozen Alpine retreats, and as many French and English provincial towns.

Returning home in the autumn of 1868 and spending the winter in lecturing, in July, 1869, he traversed the continent on the Pacific railroads, which were completed in the previous May. He called at the government posts, Fort Saunders, Fort Fred Steele, Fort Bridger and Camp Douglas. In California he explored New Almaden and the Yosemite. He went on to the Sandwich Islands in a sail vessel, made the inter-insular passage to Hilo in a schooner, and penetrated Hawaii to the crater of Kilauea.

Subsequent years Mr. B. has spent mainly in Madison, and chiefly as a student. He, however, made many domestic journeys as a railroad official. In 1878 he went abroad with his daughter Anna, and in 1884 with his daughter Agnes. On the former tour he was absent almost a year, on the latter six months. He has never ceased to preach, lecture, and write for the press.

His first lecture was "The Architecture of St. Peter's." Subsequent subjects were : "The Ceremonies of Holy Week," "Naples and its Neighborhood," "Visits to Pompeii," "Alpine Rambles," "Provincial German Life," "European Peculiarities." His most popular address was on "Common Place Books."

In the spring of 1883 he made a tour southwest to Monterey in Nuevo-Leon, the terminus at that time of railroads from the United States into Mexico. In 1887 he voyaged to Havana via. Tampa. In 1883 he camped out with three others in Yellowstone Park. They slept on the ground thirteen nights, and only twice put up their fly.

During half a century Mr. B. has corresponded for newspapers in Boston, New York, Cincinnati and Chicago. More than sixty of his articles have appeared in *The Nation*, New York. Others have come out in the Wisconsin *Academy*, the Collections of the Wisconsin Historical Society, *Lippincott*, and especially the *Bibliotheca Sacra*. Several of his sermons and educational addresses have also been printed.

His addresses before the Vermont Historical Society in 1846 on "Deficiencies in Vermont Histories," and on the "Battle of Bennington" in 1848, were the earliest publications by that association. In 1854 he was elected a member of the American An-

JAMES DAVIE BUTLER.

tiquarian Society. His address on "Pre-historic
Wisconsin" in 1876, at the annual meeting of the
State Historical Society, being the first demonstra-
tion that Wisconsin is richer than any other State
in antique implements of native copper, excited
even trans-Atlantic interest. His memorial address
in 1848 on Alexander Mitchell, the great financier
of the Northwest, was in great demand.

For four years or more onward from 1869, Mr. B.,
in the interest of a railroad that was pushing 500
miles westward from Burlington, Iowa, largely in
advance of settlement, explored, studied and described the region. His writings, in many forms
and divers languages, circulated by millions, and
were not without influence in turning the westward
stream of emigration into Nebraska.

Mary Butler (42) m. Abram Owen, Pittsford, Vt.

Their children were :

88. Mary Butler, b. 1814, June 22, m. Ebenezer
     B. Beach, Ferrisburgh.

89. Laura, b. 1815, Dec. 25, m. James Palmer.

90. Abraham, b. 1817, Oct. 26, removed to Iowa.

91. Hannah, b. 1819, Oct. 5, m. Alphonso New-
     comb.

92. James D., b. 1824, Oct. 17, d. in Ohio, 1851.

Hannah Butler (43) m. Sterns De Witt. He d.
1848, Nov. 29. She d. 1867, Dec. 19, in Oxford,
Mass.

Their children were:

88 bis. Mary, b. 1817, July 4, m. 1862, M. Freeman Freeland.

89 bis. Elizabeth, d. 1856, Sept. 27.

James D. Butler[4] (44) m. 1818, Oct. 16, Rizpah
dau. of Samuel Morgan.

93. Their son Samuel,[2] b. 1817, July 7, m. 1851,
Mary Calligan of Pittsford, Vt.

Peter H. Butler (46) m.

Their children were :

94. Celia[3], b. 1827, Nov. 12, m. James Linkmeyer,
1852, Aug. 19, Sharon. O.

95. James D.[6], b. 1830, Feb. 1, d. 1857, July 19.

96. Lucretia[2], b. 1832, Dec. 30, d. 1849, March 28.

97. Peter Glover, b. 1839, July 13, d. unm.

98. Stephen Anthony, b. 1842, Nov. 10, unm.

Jerusha Butler (48) m. Sylvester Lyon. She d.
1878. He d. 1880, Jan.

Their children were :

94 bis. Spencer C., b. 1823, June 5, d. Feb. 19,
1845.

95 bis. Mary H., 1825, bis. Jan. 13, m. James Fra-
zier, 1847, Dec. 6, d. 1848, April 27.

96 bis. Anthony L., b. 1827, April 11, d. 1838.

97 bis. Frances H., b. 1829, March 4, d. 1846,
March 30.

98 bis. Jerusha H., b. 1831, June 8, d. 1847,
March 30.

99 bis. Sarah H., b. 1833, Nov. 23, m. Dr. R. C. Hueston, 1873, Jan. 30.

100 bis. Harriet B., b. 1837, Aug. 31, m. Dr. A. W. Thompson, 1860, May 29.

101 bis. Hannah, b. 1839, Sept. 6, d. 1845, Aug. 1.

102 bis. Charles, b. 1841, April 24, m. 1867, Jan. 3, to Miss Frankie Crampton.

103 bis. James D., b. 1843, Sept. 21, m. 1870, to Miss Charlotte Owens.

104 bis. Robert L., b. 1846, July 2, m. 1885, Miss Jennie Meller.

Elizabeth Butler (50) m. Kennedy Brooks. Their children were :

105. Andrew M., b. 1831, Oct. 9.

106. Arpatia Butler, b. 1833, Jan. 21, residence, Zincite, Mo.

107. Sarah Elizabeth, b. 1834, July 31, teacher, res. Carthage, Mo.

108. Emily, b. 1836, Jan. 21, d. 1853, July 19.

109. Anthony, b. 1837, Sept. 22.

110. Robert F., b. 1839, May 8, Dr., res. Carthage, Mo.

111. Lucretia Butler, b. 1841, March 22, m. ———— Miller, Oxford, O.

112. John, b. 1843, Feb. 14, m., farmer, res. Avilla, Mo.

113. Peter H. Butler, b. 1845, Feb. 7, Dr., res. Lima, O.

114. Anna Margaret, b. 1847, Jan. 21.

Julia H. Butler (53) m. 1836, Feb. 2, Thomas
Hutchinson, M.D. He d. 1837, Sept. 11.

115. Their dau. Maria, b. 1836, Dec. 17.

Her second husband was A. B. Young, b. 1807,
May 30, d. 1884, Feb. 11.

Sarah Butler² (52) 1832, m. Benjamin F. Williams.
She d. 1868, Oct. 23.

Davie Butler Kingsbury (54) m. first Harris
———. He d. 1882, for sec. wife ———— Robinson.

His children were :

116. Jeremiah, b. 1827

117. Elizabeth, m. Rev. Henry Pratt, of Dudley,
Mass. They had a son Davie Butler
Pratt, grad. Williams Coll.

Hannah Kingsbuy (55) m. Andrew Porter

118. Their dau Elizabeth d. early.

Laura Kingsbury (56) m. Elijah Lyon.

Their children were :

119. Elizabeth Porter

120. Elijah.

Celia Butler (57) in Southbridge, m. Lement
Bacon of Woodstock, Conn. He was b. 1789, Aug.
19. He d. 1872, Nov. 19. She d. 1879, Feb. 22, in
Chelsea, Vt., where she had lived almost from the
time of her marriage.

Their children were :

121. Sarah Fisk, b. 1821, July 22, m. G. S. Harris (594)

122. Mary, b. 1823, Sept 4, m. Royal Hatch.

123. John Butler. b. 1825, Aug. 8.

124. Dana, b. 1830, April 13, of Negligh, Neb.

125. Charles, b. 1834, Aug. 8.

Susan Butler (58) Charleton, m. William Sears of Rochester, Mass.

Mary Butler (59) m. Sewall Blodgett.

John B. Bacon (123) m. Sarah Persis Morey, b. Aug. 1, 1839. Her parents M. H. Morey, b. Lyme, 1805, and Persis A. Austin, b. Concord, N. H., 1806.

Their son John Lement Bacon, b. 1862, June 18, is cashier of Bank at White River Junction.

Their two daughters were : Sarah Fisk, b. 1860, Jan. 18, d. 1860, March 13, and Mary Sigourney, b. 1865, April 23, d. 1883, Feb. 1.

James Butler (60) m. Ann Greenleaf Simpson, 1832. He d. 1874, July 30, Reading, Mass.

Their children b. in Boston, were :

126. Anne Simpson b. 1833, Jan. 30.

127. Mary Sigourney[3], b. 1835, March 17.

128. Lucy Mehitabel, b. 1836, Dec. 4.

129. Catharine. b. 1839, Aug. 16.

130. James[5], b. 1841, June 15.

131. Emily b. 1843, Sept. 5.

132. William[2], b. 1846, Mar. 9.

133. Sarah[4], b. 1849, May 8.

134. Jane, b. 1851, in Reading.

Samuel Butler (61) m. Amy Olney. He d. 1837, Dec. 16.

Their children were :

135. Mary[5], m. ——— Webb. Trempeleau, Wis.

136. James[6].

137. Emmeline, m. ——— Angell, Trempeleau, Wis.

Lucy Butler (62) m. Andrew Sigourney. (880) She d. 1876, March 14. He d. 1850, Sept. 11, in San Francisco.

Their children were :

138. Ellen E., b. 1830, May 1, m. W. F. Lloyd, . Rector in Oxford, 1863-67. She d. 1887, Feb.

139. Anne, b. 1833, July.

140. Lucy, b. 1842, Sept. 13. Both d. unm.

Mary Sigourney Butler (63) m. Samuel Stafford, of Warwick, R. I., but long resident in Providence, and then in Louisiana. She d. 1887, July 8, Worcester.

141. Their only child d. in childhood.

Her secondhusband was Andrew Porter, (see No. 118) m. 1872.

Eliza Butler (64) m. 1832, March, Wilson Olney. She d. 1874, May 2.

Their children were :

142. Richard, b. 1835, m. Agnes Thomas.

143. Peter Butler, m. Mary Butler (151)

144. George, b. ——

145. Gertrude, b. ———, m. Eben Stevens.

Sarah Butler (65) m. Edward Moore Hollman, b. 1815, May 18, Douglas, Mass. He d. 1866, Aug. 6, in Holly Springs, Miss. As a union man during the Rebellion he narrowly escaped with life and suffered great loss of property.

Their children were :

146. Clara, b. 1840, Oct. 26, Jerseyville, Ill.

147. Edward Emmons, b. 1842, Nov. 6, Jersey-
        ville.

148. Sarah, b. 1845, March 23, Douglas, Mass.

149. James Davie, b. 1849, Jan. 5, Worcester,
        Mass. Res. Washington, 1801, 9th N. W.

Peter Butler[2] (67) m. Lucia Proctor.

Their children were :

150. Lucia, b. March 25, 1846, Boston, d. 1868, Oct. 6.

151. Mary Sigourney[4], b. April 15, 1850, Boston,
        57 Bowdoin St., m. P. Butler Olney (143)

152. Isabelle J., b. Dec. 24, 1853.

153. Sigourney, b. Oct. 24, 1857, Boston, 26
        Chauncy St.

Charlotte Butler[2] (68) m. William Read Shedd, of Wells River, Vt. She d. 1885, April 12.

Their only child was :

154. Ruth Ann, b. 1854, Feb. 10th.

Peter Butler (67) long among the foremost of Boston hardware merchants, has lived for a third of a century at Quincy in the Edmund Quincy house, one of the oldest dwellings in the State, often mentioned in the journal of Judge Sewall as well as in lives of Hancock, Adams and Franklin.

A characteristic specimen of Judge Sewall's notices of the Quincy mansion is the following : (Vol. II, p. 341.)

Sixth day, March 28th, 1712. "The day and I were in a manner spent, and I turned in to Cousin Quincy where I had the pleasure to see God, in his Providence shining again upon the persons and affairs of the family, after long and distressing sickness and losses. Lodged in the chamber next the brook."

In 1885 Peter Butler was the choice of the Massachusetts democrats for the U. S. Collector at Boston. His son (153) was next year appointed second Comptroller of the U. S. Treasury. The father was made receiver of the Pacific Bank. In the spring of 1888 the dwellers in this Butler mansion had a desperate encounter with a sturdy burglar, whom they at last overpowered, bound and delivered up to justice.

RESIDENCE OF THE LATE HON. JAMES B. CAMPBELL, CHARLESTON, S. C.

Archibald Campbell (69) m. Artemeisia Wheelock. He d. 1884, May 28. She d. 1881, Dec. 16.

Their children were :

155. Archibald⁴.

156. James², b. Oct. 2.

157. Celia¹, b. 1840, d. 1862 June 14, in Columbia, S. C.

Benjamin Franklin Campbell (70) m. Mary Lilley, in Oxford, Mass. He d. 1874, March 29. She d. 1884, May 7.

Their children were :

158. Helen, b. 1833, Jan. 7.

159. Benjamin Franklin², b. 1837, Aug. 9.

160. Mary Lilley, b. 1843, Feb. 14, m. W. J. Humphrey. Their children are Celia C., b. 1872, Dec. 21, and Campbell, b. 1879, Feb. 18.

James Butler Campbell (71), m. Margaret Bennett, in Charleston, S. C. He d. 1883, Nov. 8, in Washington, D. C. She d. ——

Their children were :

161. Mary Bennett, b. ——

162. Celia². d. 1887, Feb. 28.

Celia E. Campbell (72) 1849, Oct. 4, m. Rev. S. H. Higgins, at Oxford.

163. Their child Cecil Campbell, b. 1850, Aug. 28th, m. 1887, Sept. 17, Susan Rush, in

Philadelphia. No. 163, was graduated at Princeton College. 1871. He is a lawyer, 47 Wall St., New York.

NINTH GENERATION AND THEIR CHILDREN.

Mary Elizabeth Cleveland (75) m. ―――― Johnson. Their only child was :

201. Jane, b. 1869, Sept. 24, Orinoco. Olmstead Co., Minn.

James Butler Cleveland (76) m. ――――

202. Their dau. was Catharine, b. 1864, June 14.

His second wife was Margaret Farrington, of Oneonta, N. Y., m. 1874. Sept. 29, in Washington. They have one child, George F.

Anne Butler Cleveland (77) 1834, May 18, m. Le Royal Taylor.

Their children were :

203. Annette Sophia, b. 1855, March 26.

204. Royal Cleveland, b. 1857, June 24.

205. Ella Cora, b. 1861, June 18.

206. John Wilder, b. 1866, Dec. 18.

207. Mary Alice, b. 1870, Sept. 17.

Jane Harris Cleveland (78) m. ―――― Cook, soon became a widow.

Laura Pease Cleveland (79) m. Myron Manly of Lawrence, Kansas.

Their only child was :

208. Robbie, b. 1868, July 20.

James D. Butler[6] (95) m. —— Bevis.

208 bis. Their son Calvin Bevis, b. 1856, Jan. 20.

Eliza Lyon (99) 1839, March 21, m. R. H. Bishop, Oxford, O.

Their children were :

209. Mary Jane.

210. Emily.

211. Catharine.

212. George.

214. Sylvester.

215. Anna.

216. Helen.

217. Peter.

217 bis. Mary.

218. Julia.

219. Lucy.

Andrew M. Brooks (105) m.

Their children were :

220. Kennedy b. 1856.

221. Mary, b. 1858.

222. James, b. 1860.

223. Maggie, b. 1864.

224. Annie, b. 1868.

225. Fanny, b. 1870.

226. Andrew, b. Nov., 1874.

226 bis. Alice, 1877.

Maria Hutchinson (115) m 1857, John Baker.
Their children were :

220 bis. Benjamin W.

221 bis. Edgar Hughes.

222 bis. Samuel W.

223 bis. Julia Florence, b. 1876.

No. (220) grad. Worcester, O. is lawyer in Hamilton, O.

Sarah Bacon (121) m. 1845, Feb. 12. George Samuel Harris (594) who was b. 1815, March 22, d. 1874, June 12, Lincoln, Nebraska.

Their children were :

227. Celia Elizabeth, b. South Bend (Ind), 1846, April 2, No. 723 bis.

228. George Bacon, b. 1848, Dec. 20.

229. Susan Ellen, b. Boston, 1851, Feb. 3, d. 1866, Hannibal.

230. Charles Leonard, b. Boston, 1853, Nov. 4, m. 1883, Jan. 17, Mary E. Day.

231. Mary Germaine, b. 1855, July 7, d. 1857, Chelsea, Vt.

232. Frederick Lement, b. 1857, Oct. 11, West Roxbury, Mass. See 735.

233. Edward Kirk, b. Boston, 1859, April 21.

234. Sarah Butler, b. Boston, 1860, July 18.

235. John Francis, b. Boston, 1863, Feb. 24.

236. Agnes Butler, b. Hannibal, 1866, Feb. 20, d. the same day.

Mary Bacon (122) m. Royal Hatch.

Their children were :

237. Edward L., b. 1857, Strafford, Vt., d. 1884, Negligh, Neb.

G. S. Harris (121) Land Commissioner of the Burlington and Missouri River Railroad from 1869 to '74 contributed largely to the industrial development of Nebraska. In 1872, he was on board the *Metis*, a steamer wrecked on Long Island Sound. When the vessel sank he floated off on a door, and was rescued after some hours. But though surviving for more than two years he never fully recovered from the exposure. His escape from drowning was singularly like that of his father's cousin, Samuel Harris (513).

G. B. Harris (228) in 1887, building the Burlington and Northern railroad became famous for finishing three hundred miles of track with unexampled skill and celerity.

Anne S. Butler (126) m. G. W. Gouard.

Their children were :

238. Jessie, b. 1860, Oct.

239. George Henry, b. 1861, July 27

Mary S. Butler[1] (127) m. Augustus Hood. He d. 1867.

240. Their dau. Mary, m. Hatch, 1885, Dec. 6.

Lucy M. Butler (128) m. Frank H. Smith.

Their son is:

241. Frank.

6

Catharine Butler(229) m. Sidney L. Smith.
Their son is:
242. Philip Sidney, b. 1877.
James Butler[6] (130) m. Caroline Orel.
Emily Butler (131) m. Fred. W. Flint.
William Butler[2] (132) m. Hattie Nash.
Sarah Butler[3] (133).

Jane Butler (134) d. Reading, 1871.

Ellen Sigourney (138) m. Rev. W. F. Lloyd in
Oxford. She d. 1887, Feb.

Their children were :
257. Irwin, b. 1868, Oct. 18.
252. William, b. ———.
253. Percy Butler, b. 1872, Feb. 11.

Richard Olney (142) m. Agnes Thomas.
Their children were .
254.
255.

Peter B. Olney (143) m. Mary Butler (151) 1879,
Nov. 12, in Quincy, Mass. Lives New York City,
9th street, No. 16.

Their children were :
256. Peter Butler, b. 1881, April 9.
257. Richard, b. 1883, Feb.24.
258. Wilson, b. 1885, Aug. 18.

George Olney (144) m.
Gertrude Olney (144) m. Eben Stevens.

TENTH GENERATION.

Catherine Cleveland (202) 1883, Jan. 24, m. L. E. Harris, Franklin, N. Y.

278. Their son Stanley C., b. 1887, Jan 22.

Calvin Bevis Butler (208 bis,) m. 1879, Sept. 8, Venora L. Whitlock. In hardware firm, Homer, Ill.

Their children are:
279. Mary M.
280. Roxy A.
281. Laura B.

Emily Bishop (210) m. D. J. Vance.
Their children are:
282 Julia.
283. Margaret.

George Bishop (212) m. Virginia Patterson.
Their child is:
284. Maria Speer.

Robert Bishop (213) m. Kate Thompson.
Their children are:
285. Robert
286. Thompson.
287. Harry.
288. Kate.

Maria Hutchinson (115) m. —— Baker
Their son B. W. Baker, m.————. Has a son John Calvin, b. 1886.

James D. Butler (41) m. Anna Bates (334).

Regarding the lineage of Anna Bates my gleanings are as follows :

300. Clement Bates[1], b. in England, County Kent
or Suffolk, in 1595, was m. to Ann ———.

Their children were :

301. James[1], b. 1621.

302. Clement[2], b. 1623.

303. Rachel, b. 1627.

304. Joseph[1], b. 1630.

305. Benjamin, b. 1633.

306. Samuel, b. ———

In 1635 on the ship *Elizabeth* he arrived in
Hingham in New England, with his wife, five
children, two servants, and James Bates[2], perhaps
his brother. By occupation he was a tailor. Land
was allotted him in Hingham.

Joseph Bates (304) in 1659, m. Esther Hilliard.

Their children were :

307. Joseph[2].

308. Caleb.

309. Hannah[1].

310. Joshua, b. 1666 ca.

311. Bathsheba.

312. Clement[3].

313. Eleazar.

Joshua Bates(310) m. Abigail ———.
Among their children was :

314. Joshua[2], b. 1695 ca, m. Abigail ———
Among their children was :

315. Joshua[3]. b. 1725, m. Grace Lincoln.
Among their children was :

316. Zealous, b. 1754, m. Abigail Nichols. He d.
1834.

Their children were :

317. Joshua[4], b. 1776, March 20, m. Anna Poor.

318. Daniel, b. 1778, Jan. 21.

319. Abigail[1], b. 1780, Aug. 6.

320. Paul, b. 1781, Aug. 10.

321. David, b. 1784, Sept. 12.

322. Anna[1], b. 1787, March 22, m. Tower.

323. Phineas, b. 1790, April 24.

324. Abigail[2], b, 1792 Jan. 22, m. Otis Brigham.

325. Jane[1], b. 1794, April 3, m. ——— Fay.

326. Adeline, b. 1801, May 10, m. Otis Brigham.

Anna Poor (above) was dau. of Daniel Poor and
his wife Hannah Frye, and b. Andover, 1783, Feb.
28.

Joshua Bates (317) 1804, Sept. 4, m. Anna Poor.

He d. 1854, Jan. 14. She d. 1826, Feb. 7, Middlebury, Vt.

Their children, the first eight, b. in Dedham, Mass., the others in Middlebury, Vt., were :

327. Mary, b. 1805, June 15.

328. Hannah[2], b. 1807, Feb. 15.

329. Abby, b. 1808, Dec. 1.

330. Joshua[5], b. 1810, March 17.

331. John Codman, b. 1812, Nov. 5.

332. Prentiss, b. 1814, May 16.

333. William, b. 1816, Jan. 18.

334. Anna[2], b. 1818, Jan. 30.

335. Jane[2], b. 1819, Oct. 24.

336. Samuel W.[1], b. 1822, Nov. 9.

337. Agnes, b. 1824, Sept. 5.

Joshua Bates (317) 1827. Feb. 8, m. Maria S. Latimer, b. 1786, d. 1855, Aug. 12.

338. Their child Maria, b. 1828, Aug 9, d. 1862, Nov. 19.

Hannah Bates (328) 1833. Sept. 16, m. Henry Smith, b. 1805 Dec. 16. He d. 1879 Jan'y 14, Cincinnati, O.

Their children were b. in Marietta, Ohio:

339. Henry Kirk, b. 1834 July 10.

340. Albert Linnekogel, b. 1841 Feb. 24, d. 1858 Sep. 8, Greenwich, Conn.

341. Frederick Bates, b. 1843 Jan'y 23, m. Katharine Fuller.

Joshua Bates (330), m. Lucy How, b. on Fort Hill, Boston, 1823 June 12. He d. Beverly, Mass., 1888, June.

Abby Bates (329), d. Middlebury Vt. 1849 Aug. 27.

342. Their son Frank Cornelius, b. 1863 Sept. 12.

John C. Bates (330), 1845 May, m. Sarah Tagliaferro. He d. 1857, Sept. 22.

343. Their dau. Elizabeth, b. 1846 Feb. 7, m. John Garrett.

Agnes Bates (337) d. Charleston, S. C., 1869, Feb. 15.

William Bates (333) 1848, June 8, in Northampton Mass. m. Cornelia Lee, b. 1826, Dec., Conway, Mass. He d. 1859, Sep. 10, Falmouth, Mass.

Their children were :
344. Arthur Lee, b. 1851, March 25, Northbridge, Mass.
345. Jane[3], b. 1854, July 6, Northbridge, Mass.
346. Samuel[2] Lee, b. 1857, Feb 25,   "
347. Kate Lee, b. 1859, Aug. 12, Falmouth, Mass. Graduated at Wellesly College, 1880, and became Professor there.

Anna Bates (335) m. James D. Butler (10).

Jane Bates (335) m. Jas. Cobb, M. D., San Jose, Cal. He d. 1872, April 5.

Samuel Bates (336) 1855, Sept. 19, m. Annie How, b. 1835, March 25, South Boston. He d. 1882, Jan. 13.

Their children were:

348. Waldron, 1856, Nov. 26.

349. Samuel W.[2] 1858, Oct. 20.

350. Charles How, 1868, Feb. 23.

Arthur Lee Bates (344) m. 1881, Oct. 17, Newton-
ville, Mass. to Nellie Gertrude Bean, b. 1857, March
25, Boston.

Their dau. Elizabeth Frances, b. 1886, January 7,
Portland, Me.

Samuel L. Bates (346) m. 1882, Aug. 2, Philadelphia, Mary Sloan Smith, b. 1863, Aug. 2.

Maria Bates (338) m. Joseph Warner. She died
1862, Nov. 19. Mr. W.'s children by a former marriage were:

James, Mary, Ezra.

Henry Smith, m. Hannah Bates (328). He was b.
1805, Dec. 16, in Milton, Vt. of parents both of
whom were natives of Bennington. He graduated
at Middlebury in 1827 and at Andover in 1833. In
October of the same year he became classical professor in Marietta, O., and in 1846 he was elected
President of Marietta College. In 1855 he removed
to Lane Seminary and continued there till his death
in 1879, except about four years, during which he
was pastor in Buffalo, N. Y. Prof. Smith in 1836,
went abroad and studied a year in German universities. He crossed the Atlantic often and once
traveled as far as Jerusalem. He never ceased to
preach and lecture. Many of his occasional sermons were published. His translation of the

Homeric lexicon of Crusius came out in 1844, and
his critical essay on Spinoza, a volume of 500 pages,
was issued after his death.   He is buried at Marietta, in Oak Grove cemetery.

Prentiss Bates (332) became insane about 1838 ;
was placed in the Brattleborough Hospital and has
remained there a half century.

The same infirmity has shown itself in David (321)
and Mary (327).

Joshua Bates (317) in 1797, entered Sophomore in
Harvard College.   He taught school two winters
during his college course, and began a third school,
but was obliged by illness to relinquish it.   Among
his classmates were, Allston—the painter, Buckminster, afterwards Pastor of Brattle street church,
and chief justice Lemuel Shaw.   At graduation in
1800, the class numbered forty seven, and Mr. Bates
was its valedictorian.   His oration was on, "The
progress of Refinement."   In the catalogue of the
British Museum I have counted twenty-eight titles
of sermons and other works published by him and
now in the library of that institution.   Nearly as
many titles appear in Sprague's American Congregational Pulpit.

In 1803, March 16, Mr. B., became pastor in
Dedham, Mass.   In the spring of 1818, he left that
pulpit and was inaugurated President of Middlebury college.   Resigning that position in 1839, he
was elected Congressional Chaplain.   On leaving
Washington he was installed pastor in Dudley,

Mass., 1843, Mar. 22, where he continued to preach till his death in 1854.

At his grave in Middlebury, Vt., there is a monument with this inscription : [On the east face]. In testimony of love and honor to one who trained and educated four hundred and fifty of their number, by the Alumni of Middlebury college. [On the north face.] Graduated with highest honors at Harvard College, 1800 ; Pastor at Dedham, Mass., 1803–18 ; Chaplain of 26th Congress ; Pastor at Dudley, Mass., 1843–54. [On the west face]. Gracious and faithful as a christian pastor, he rests in God, while his life and work still live in those he trained, an imperishable legacy to the age. [On the south face]. President of Middlebury College 1818–39. Born at Cohassett, Mass., March 20, 1776. Died at Dudley, Mass., Jan'y 14, 1854.

Beside him are buried both his wives and four of their children.

At the semi-centennial celebration of Middlebury College, in August 1850. Dr. Bates, the ex-president, addressed the Alumni. At their dinner one of the speakers was John G. Saxe, who delivered a poem in which the following lines related to Dr. Bates.

> Ah ! well I remember the President's face,
> As he sat at the lecture with dignified grace,
> And neatly unfolded the mystical themes
> Of various deep metaphysical schemes :
> How he brightened the path of his studious flock,
> As he gave them the key to that wonderful *Locke ;*

How he taught us to feel it was fatal indeed,
With too much reliance, to lean upon *Reid ;*
How *Stewart* was sounder, but wrong at the last,
From following his master a little too fast,
Then closed the discourse in a scholarly tone,
With a clear and intelligent creed of his own
That the man had his faults it were safe to infer ;
Though I really don't recollect what they were ;
I barely remember this one little truth,
When his case was discussed by the critical youth,
The Seniors and Freshmen were sure to divide,
And the former were all on the President's side.

I read the following record in the class-book of
class of 1800, in Harvard College. Page 12 :

Bates, Joshua, of Cohasset, b. 20 March 1776, fitted
for college by Rev. Josiah C. Shaw; entered a year in
advance with Cabot, Lowell, Sanger, Buckminster,
graduated with first part. Assistant one year at
Phillips Academy, Andover. Studied at Dedham,
1803, m. Miss Nancy Poor, of Andover. President
of Middlebury College, 1818. Resigned 1839. Chaplain of U. S. Representatives 1839, 1840. Preached
two years at Northborough, went thence to Dudley,
installed March 22, 1843, being 40 years from time
of ordination at Dedham. Sermons of his published, and letters from Washington in *Recorder ;*
and in 1846, Lectures on Christian Character, in
one vol. 8vo. Widower 1826. Re-married to Miss
Maria S. Latimer, of Middletown, Conn., had 13
children by first marriage ; one by second; seven sons
and seven daughters, two sons died infants. D. D.
Yale ; engaged in farming and merchandise till

about two years before entering college and kept school one year before entering. Procured funds for education by taking sixty muskrats, then let out the proceeds on sheep in shares : before entering college made $270. Two sons instructors, three daughters instructors, two m. college teachers; one son lawyer, one clergyman. Died at Dudley, 14 Jan., '54, inflammation of kidneys.

This Class Book was received by Harvard College 8 March, 1870, as the gift of the class of 1800.

Posted on the front fly-leaf is the following written note :-

" This Class book was kept by me for the use of the Harvard University and Library and is to be delivered to their Librarian as soon as the last of the Class is no more. S. SWETT.

Forty-seven of the class graduated. Ten others at different times were members of the Class, but left before graduating.

Mr. Bates would never have had a liberal educa tion but for a misfortune, an accidental wound in his right wrist made it impossible to open and shut his hand fully. Hence incapaciated for manual labor he was forced to the bettering of his mind. That the defect in his hand might not be noticed, his habit was in public speaking to hold in his hand a book or handkerchief.

Joshua Bates (330) was graduated at Middlebury college in 1832. He dedicated his life to teaching, first in Charlestown, Mass., and then in Boston, where he was master of the Brimmer school till he became the Dean of all the metropolitan masters.

John C. Bates (331) was graduated at Middlebury in 1834. He went south, taught awhile, but in 1840 became editor of the Alabama [Whig] *Journal* at Montgomery, and continued in this work till his death in Sept., 1857.

William Bates (333) graduated at Middlebury, in 1837, and at Andover in 1840. He was a Congregational minister. He was settled first in Northbridge, Mass., and then in Falmouth, where he was pastor at his death in 1859.

Samuel W. Bates (336) graduated at Middlebury, in 1843. He was at first master of one of the Boston public schools, but turning to the law, became eminent, especially in Patent and Railroad specialties.

Mary Bates (327) after some teaching in Woodstock, Vt., in 1838, established a seminary in Pendleton, S. C., under the patronage of J. C. Calhoun. She set up a branch in Tallahassee (Fla.), but at length confined her teaching altogether to Charleston. Her establishment here, with the co-operation of her sisters, was a power for good till long after the siege began. With her sister Agnes she then escaped to Europe, where she had traveled before. When the war was well over, the sisters returned to their work in Charleston. Nor did they cease from it till the utter failure of their health. Miss Mary printed a good booklet on the private life of John C. Calhoun.

HARRISIANA.

James D. Butler[4] (28) m. widow Rachel *Harris* Maynard.

Regarding the lineage of this Rachel Harris, born 1775, Williamstown, Mass., the following particulars have been ascertained. The facts regarding several generations backward from 1740 I owe to Mr. Frank Fansworth Starr, of Middletown, Ct.

SUMMARY OF HARRIS LINEAGE.

450. — Thomas Harris m. Elizabeth ———.

461. Their son Daniel, b. 1618 or soon after, m. Mary Weld.

463. Their son Daniel, b. 1653, m. Abigail Barnes.

475. Their son Daniel, b. 1688, m. Abigail ———.

502. Their son John[6], b. 1720, m. Rachel Moss.

505. Their son Israel, b. 1747, m. Sarah Morse.

511. Their daughter Rachel, b. 1775, m. James D. Butler (28).

FIRST GENERATION.

450. Thomas Harris[1], m. Elizabeth ———, b. 1576. He died before 1633. She died 1669, Feb. 16, aged 93.

Their children were :

451. John[1].

452. Thomas[2].

453. William[1].

461. Daniel[1].

In 1680 Dea. William Stilson testified in court that Thomas Harris (450) kept the ferry from Boston to Winnisimmet and Charlestown, forty-nine years ago [1631], that he himself had married the widow of Harris and continued the ferry. (Wyman, Charlestown Estates. p. 467.) Deacon S. at his death in 1691, left property to four sons of his wife Elizabeth by Thomas Harris (450) namely : John, Thomas, William and Daniel. (Frothingham, p. 87.) Stilson and his wife Elizabeth were admitted to the church in Charlestown in 1633, March 22. Forty-seven descendants of Thomas Harris (450) are described by Wyman in Charlestown, though all but one of his sons removed elsewhere.

SECOND GENERATION.

461. Daniel Harris¹. b. ca. 1618, son of Thomas (450), who lived in Charlestown, Mass., in 1648 [Savage], m. Mary Weld, dau. of Joseph and Elizabeth Weld, of Roxbury. Mary Weld, b. 1627, in England, perhaps in Terling,᾽ Co. Essex, 38 miles from London ; was in 1635 brought by her parents to Roxbury, where her father's brother Thomas was minister. The will of Joseph Weld, who d. 1646, is very noteworthy. [Gen. Reg., VII, p. 33.] Real estate bequeathed by him to Mrs. Mary Harris. she sold for £35, May 19, 1652. (Suffolk Deeds.)

In 1643 Daniel Harris (461) had settled in Rowley, about 35 miles north of Boston. He was by trade a wheelwright. In 1652 he sold out and removed to

Middletown, Conn. There he located his five-acre homestead, on the east side of Main street, a few rods south of the present College street, and extending east to the "Great River." "At a session of the General Court, held Feb. 23, 1659, Daniel Harris is approved for an ordinary keeper in Middletown." In 1677 he was elected Captain of the train-band [had been a Lieutenant in 1661]. He was deputy to the General Court in 1678-84-87-89. He d. 1708, Nov. 30. His wife d. 1711, Sept. 5, aged 84.

Their children were :

462. Mary[1], b. April 2, 1651, Rowley.

463. Daniel, b. July 16, 1653, Middletown.

464. Joseph[1], b. Feb. 12, 1654, Middletown. He d. young.

465. Thomas[3], b. May 20, 1657, Middletown. Mary, his only child.

466. Elizabeth[1], b. March 22, 1659, Middletown.

467. Sarah[1], b. 17 Feb., 1660, Middletown.

468. Sarah[2], b. Sept. 30 1663, Middletown.

469. William[2], b. July 17 1665, Middletown.

470. John[2], b. Jan'y 4 1667, Middletown.

471. Hannah[1], b. Feb. 11, 1669, Middletown.

THIRD GENERATION.

Daniel Harris[2] (463), 1680, Dec. 14, m. Abigail Barnes, Middletown. He d. 1735, Oct. 18. She d. 1723, May 22.

Their children were :

472. Abigail, b. 1682-3.

473. Mary², b. 1685.

474. Elizabeth², b.

475. Daniel³, b. 1688, Oct.

476. Joseph², b. 1691, March 1.

477. Patience, b. 1693, May 15.

478. Elizabeth³, b.

The second wife of Daniel (463) m. 1726-7, Jan. 5, was Elizabeth (Bedell) Cook, widow of Samuel Cook, of Wallingford. Daniel Harris (463), d. at the age of eighty-two, and was buried in the oldest burying ground of Middletown, where his monument is still to be seen. In March 1742–3, his widow Elizabeth was living in Wallingford, after this date all trace of her is lost.

Joseph Harris (476), b. 1691, in April 1721, purchased lands in Litchfield, and the same year removed there from Middletown, where he had sold his lands for £440. His farm was at the north end of West Plains, near Myron Osborn's house. While at work there he was shot and scalped by Indians in August 1723. His widow Mary, b. 1700, in 1725, Dec. 16, m. Stephen Sedgwick. His daughter Abigail m. Asa Hopkins, of Litchfield. He was interred in the West burying-ground. Over his remains there is a monument with this inscription.

"In memory of Joseph Harris, who was murdered by the Indians, in August 1721 [mistake for 1723, as in Dec. 1722, he was elected collector], while plowing in his field about three-fourths of a mile

7

west of the graveyard. He was shot by Indians concealed in ambush. He was found dead, sitting on the ground, his head and body reclined against the trunk of a tree. To record the first death among the original settlers, and to perpetuate the memory of a worthy but unfortunate citizen, this monument is erected in 1830 ; by the voluntary benefactions of individual subscribers."

This tribute was written by Truman Marsh, an Episcopal minister. (J. W. Barber, *Hist. Collections*, p. 454.)

A grandson of Joseph, (476) Seth Harris, who before had lived in Kingsbury, N. Y., in 1810, became a partner of John Harris (504) the scythe-maker. Seth's sons, John and Silas continued the manufacture, and their scythes,- thanks not only to their excellence but to the business aptitudes of Silas had no rivals on the Hudson, or in New England. Particulars concerning this manufacture and John Harris (504) gathered by Mr. Isaac Huntting, of Pine Plains were published in 1881, in the Pough-keepsie *Telegraph*.

The children of Daniel Harris (475) and his wife Abigail ——— :

479. Miriam, b. 1713, July.

480. Daniel⁴, b. 1715, April 10.

481. Moses, b. 1717, May 20.

502. John³, b. 1719–20, Feb. 26.

482. Thomas⁴, b. 1722, May 9.

483. Abigail, b.

484. Joseph³, b.

485. Joshua, b. 1729. Sept. 3.

486. Gilbert. b. 1735. June 7.

Daniel Harris (475) m. Abigail. Her birth, parentage and date of marriage are unknown. He resided in Middletown, till about 1727, and then purchased a hundred acre lot in Wallingford where he was residing in September, 1729. In February, 1738, he bought one right in the new town of Goshen, Litchfield Co., and removed there in the spring of 1739, being then fifty years old. Before June, 1756, his home was in Cornwall, but no later notices concerning him have been detected.

Moses (481) and Gilbert (486) as soldiers at the taking of Port Royal (?), in the war of 1754-63, and so entitled to land bounty were Washington Co. pioneers on Bradshaw's Patent.

FIFTH GENERATION.

Moses Harris (481). m. ———. He is said to have d. in Kentucky.

Their children whose names are known were :

482 bis. Moses, Jr., b. 1748, Nov. 19.

483 bis. William³, b.

484 bis. Joseph, b.

In June, 1775, the name of Moses H., Jr. (482) appears in the list of associates in Amenia precinct, of Dutchess Co., where his father (481) appears as a

lead miner the next year. From 1776 to 1781, he
was a spy or secret service agent between New York
and Canada. After the Revolution he had an
annual pension of $96, and it is believed a land-
bounty. He was a land surveyor. His traditionary
adventures are detailed in Dr. Holden's *History of
Queensbury*. The region south-east of Lake George,
where with his brothers Joseph and William, he
settled in June, 1787, was directly named Harrisana.
His uncle Joshua (485) also had land there. After
the Revolution his uncle Gilbert (486) a tory, taking
refuge on the west of Lake George, died in Bolton.
Moses, Jr. (482 bis), d. at Harrisana, 1838, Nov. 13,
lacking but one week of being a monagenarian.

His son Moses, b. 1775, had a son named John J.
Harris.

Moses H., Sr. (481), in 1780 (?) with his son
William (483 bis) was seized by Indians at the house
of his brother Gilbert (486). Both were carried to
Canada, and suffered great hardships on the march.

John Harris (502), b. in Middletown, when ten
years old removed with parents (475) to Wallingford. Ten years afterward he was m. in 1740, to
Rachel Moss, in Derby, where he resided for five
years. In the Summer of 1745, he settled in Goshen,
and the next year passed on into the adjoining town
of Cornwall, where he was one of the first deacons in
the Congregational church. In November, 1751, he
had already removed to Little Nine Partners, that is.
the Oblong, Dutchess Co., N. Y. Tradition through

Isaac Huntting, of Pine Plains, Dutchess county,
gives his residence as on the Lawrence place, in the
town of North East, near Spencer's Corners in the
present town of North East. But he did not own
it nor any other land in Dutchess Co. The exact
date of his death has not been ascertained. It is
certain however, that his widow, Rachel, on May
27, 1760, was m. in Salisbury, Conn., to David
Owen, as his second wife, and on Jan. 8, 1762, said
Owen was appointed "guardian of Israel Harris
(505) aged fourteen on the 27 of last February, son
of John Harris, late of the Oblong,deceased." The
record is to be found in Sharon Probate office, a
district which included Salisbury. The first church
in the Oblong was organized in 1740. If its records
are extant they may contain notice of John Harris
or his children. In 1762 mention is made of Owen's
(Leonard) Iron Works in Salisbury, which were
then sold to Ethan Allen and others John Owen
of Salisbury, was a soldier in the French war. In
1753, the Moravian visitor Abraham Reinke,
preached some weeks in a meeting-house, midway
between the house of John Harris and Sharon
village,—about two miles from each. In the autumn of that year he carried to the Board in Beth-
lehem, a petition for a preacher to be sent to them
"subscribed by thirty-four of his stated hearers."
Among them was John Harris. This John Harris
was buried either in the Moravian cemetery near
Round Top church, or more probably in a burial

ground of the Harris family,— the remains in which were afterwards transferred to the public cemetery of Pine Plains, just north of the village.

John Harris[4] (502), m. 1740-41, Feb. 5, Rachel Moss.

Among their children were :

503. Timothy, b. 1742, Oct. 6, Derby, Conn.

504. John[5], 1744-5, March 5, Derby, Conn.

505. Israel[2], b. 1746-7, Feb. 16, Cornwall, Conn.

506. Rachel[2], b. 1749, Feb. 22, Cornwall, Conn.

507. Samuel[1], b. Oblong, North-east precinct.

It was related by Lois (522) that Rachel (506) m. Joseph Hawkins, who had been a gun-smith in the British army and that their children were : John, Samuel, Joseph and Benjamin (twins), William, Deborah, and Rachel who m. McNeil Seymour.

SIXTH GENERATION.

John Harris (504) m. Mary Gamble. She was b. 1752, Westchester Co. He d. 1814, Nov. 27. She d. 1834, Dec. 20.

Their children were :

487. Anne, m. Henry Knapp, Broome Co., N. Y.

488. Israel[1], m. Phebe Barker, dau. Wm. Barker of Amenia.

489. James[1], not m.

490. Polly m. ——— Thompson.

491. Rachel[1], m. ——— Lapham, Penn Yan.

492. Lois¹, m. Periam Thompson, nephew of Polly's.

493. Elizabeth¹, b. 1788, July 25.

494. Eunice, m. Cyrus Burnap, no child.

495. Hannah, m. John W. Righter, Pine Plains.

John Harris (504) b. 1745, in Derby, Conn., as an infant was brought to Cornwall and thence into the Oblong, Dutchess Co., N. Y. He was brought up a blacksmith there, and learned to make scythes of a mulatto slave, owned by his Uncle Joseph (484) who according to tradition lived in Rhode Island.

In 1770 he settled near Ft. Ann, a post established in 1756, 67 miles north of Albany. In the spring of 1777, through fear of Indians he fled with an ox-sled of moveables, and looking backward saw his house in flames kindled by Indians. His wife with two children, the oldest but three years old, had started sooner on horseback. He settled in Amenia precinct, Great Nine Partners, at Andrus Rowe corners. In 1783 he moved to Harris Mills, Pine Plains, north-east precinct, where on Dec. 19, he bought a place for £420, which in 1810 he conveyed to his son Israel. In 1787 he paid for the adjacent mill-site £150.

Elizabeth Harris (493) m. James G. Husted, b. 1788, August 22, on a farm near Pine Plains, that in 1858 had been six generations in the Husted family. Her portrait hangs there, and is well

painted. Her physique and expression — blonde,
with dark eyes, wearing a cap,—with a book and
glasses in her hand—are of the same type with other
branches of the Harris race.

496. Seth Harris a grandson of Joseph (476) m.
    Isabella Gamble. She d. before 1810.

Their children were :

497. John³, b. ———

498. Silas, b. 1787, Jan. 24, d. 1862, April 19.

199. Elizabeth, b. ———, (a belle) m. Barnum
    of Salisbury.

John Harris (504) and his wife were among the
first seven members of the First Methodist church
at its organization in 1785. Class meetings were
held at his saw-mill house. The seats were of slabs.

Regarding the descent of Rachel Moss who m.
John Harris (502) I find as follows : About 1639
John Moss was among the pioneers at New Haven.
His son Joseph in 1667 m. Mary Alling. Joseph's
son Israel, b. 1684, ca. in 1717 m. Lydia Bowers in
Derby, Conn. Their dau. Rachel, b. 1719, Jan. 24,
m. 1740, John Harris (502).

Israel Harris² (505) m. Sarah Morse. He d. 1836
Nov. 28. She d. 1833, Dec. 25. Both d. in South
    Hartford, [N. Y.

Their children were :

508. John⁶, b. 1771, Jan. 5.

509. Elizabeth⁶, b. 1772.

510. Sarah³, b. 1773.

511. Rachel[3], b. **1775**, April 2, Williamstown, Mass. m. Butler (28)

512. Israel[3], b. **1776**, Dec. 31, Williamstown.

513· Samuel[2], b. **1778**, Feb. 17, Williamstown.

514. Joseph[1] b. **1779**, Feb. 1. Williamstown.

515. Timothy[2], b. **1781**, March 15, Williamstown.

516. Lois[2], b. **1783**, Jan. 25, Rutland, Vt.

517. Chloe, b. ―――― Rutland, Vt. She d. 1808. April 24.

The family of the above mentioned Sarah Morse, which appears at New Haven in 1638, removed to Wallingford, Conn. in 1677. John Morse who d. 1707 had a son John, b. 1650 Oct. 12 who in 1677 m. Mary Lathrop. Their fifth child Solomon b. 1690 July 9, m. in 1714 Ruth Peck. Their fourth child Solomon b. 1719. d. Nine Partners, m. Elizabeth Fenn, 1743 Nov. 30. Their dau. Sarah m. Israel Harris (512). Her brothers Amasa, Joseph and Solomon, were revolutionary soldiers under her husband as Captain.

There is probably a mistake in the year of the birth of Samuel (513). The year may have been 1780.

Israel Harris (505) is said to have been brought up as a carpenter, and a maker of foot spinning wheels. At the outbreak of the Revolution he was twenty eight years old, had a wife and four children, the oldest less than six years old. He was then living rather distant from neighbors in the northwest corner of Massachusetts at Williamstown. In

1775 early in May he joined Allen's force as it passed through Williamstown.   He entered Ticonderoga
with Allen on the morning of May 10th.   According to his report the first summons of Allen to the
British commander was : " Come out here you d—d
old rat !"   He speedily returned to his wife whose
infant Rachel,—my mother, was but a few weeks
old.   Before the end of May he had enlisted for six
months, and was orderly sergeant in Col. Eason's
command which built boats at Ticonderoga, sailed
in August to St. Johns, and captured it in December.   He was then mustered out.   The next October (1777) he was mustered in at Williamstown, as
orderly sergeant under Captain Smedly, and served
at Ticonderoga four months.   In 1777, about the
first of July, under Capt. Samuel Clark he marched
to Fort Ann.   Fought Burgoyne's men there one
day successfully, on the second day was forced to
retreat to Fort Edward.   Returning home on fur-
lough, he was within a week ordered out again
among the minute men, and served as lieutenant
[or perhaps was still orderly sergeant], in the
battle of Bennington, Aug. 16.   He was in the
party which on that day stormed the intrenchment
of Peter's corps of Tories.   Allowed to go home,
probably for harvesting, he was again, before the
end of August, in the field.   Stationed first in Pawlet, he then moved through Weils and along the
frontier to Whitehall.   In this movement for cutting off Burgoyne's northern communications he

was Lieut. under Captain Jude Williams. In May 1778 as Lieut. under Col. Wood, after some recruiting, he was encamped at Peekskill, marched thence to White Plains,—and so eastward to Farmington on Connecticut River,—keeping pace with the British advance on Long Island. Returning to Peeskill was discharged there the next Feb. 1779.

In May 1779 as captain of the second company in Col. Simonds regiment he served three months on the Vermont frontier. These details are mainly derived from the Pension claim here following of Israel Harris still on file in the U. S. Pension office, Washington.

PENSION CLAIM.—Israel Harris, of Salem, Washington Co., N. Y., August 2⁹, 1832, states that he is eighty five years old ; that he entered the service of the United States under the following-named officers, and served at the times and in the manner herein stated, as well as after the lapse of time he recollects, to-wit :

"In May, 1775, volunteered under Colonel Ethan Allen, to march with a party of volunteers and seize upon the fortress of Ticonderoga. Marched from Williamstown in Massachusetts,to Castleton in Vermont. Thence to Ticonderoga, in New York, and entered the fortress at that place on the morning of May 10. In a few days returned home to Williamstown, aforesaid.

"About the last of May, 1775, enlisted as orderly sergeant into the company commanded by Captain

Lemuel Steward, Lieutenant Ezekiel Blair and
Second Lieutenant Nathan Smith (for the term of
six months), attached to the regiment of Massachusetts State troops commanded by field officers
Colonel James Eason, Major John Brown.   Same
month said regiment commanded by Colonel Eason,
marched to Fort Ticonderoga, aforesaid, and commenced building boats for an excursion northward.
In August following, the whole army, consisting of
four regiments commanded by Brigadier-General
Montgomery, sailed from Ticonderoga to St. Johns,
in Canada, and laid siege to the fortress so called.
Said siege lasted three months and four days, when
the garrison surrendered to General Montgomery on
the 4th day of December, 1775.   Towards the close
of December Colonel Eason's regiment was discharged at St. Johns, whence they proceeded to
their homes.

   "Was ordered, in the first part of October, 1776,
as orderly sergeant in the company of militia commanded by Captain N. Smedley, Lieutenant Jude
Williams, and Second Lieutenant Timothy Bigelow,
to muster at Williamstown, aforesaid.   Said company belonged to a regiment of militia commanded
by Colonel Simonds of Williamstown aforesaid.
Said company marched to Ticonderoga, in New
York, and said Israel Harris continued there in
person and by substitute, at his own expense, four
months, at the expiration of which time said company was dismissed,and returned home in January.

"About the 1st of July, 1777, marched as orderly sergeant in Colonel Simonds' regiment of militia in the company commanded by Captain Samuel Clark, from Williamstown, Massachusetts, to Fort Ann, in the county of Washington, New York. In the vicinity of said fort they encountered a detachment of General Burgoyne's army, and a severe engagement ensued, in which the enemy were routed and driven back. On the following day, the British having been reënforced, another severe engagement was fought, which resulted in the retreat of Colonel Simonds to Fort Edward, in said county. General Schuyler, being commander-in-chief, ordered one-half of Simonds' regiment to return home (in which was included said Israel Harris), to hold themselves in readiness to march at a minute's warning.

"About one week after, a detachment of the British army, under the command of Colonel Baum, advanced to Bennington, in Vermont. In the mean time Colonel Simonds had returned home, when he received an express from General Schuyler with orders to take the field with all the force he could muster, and forthwith march to Bennington to oppose Baum. The said Harris was included in the muster, and subsequently, upon the 16th of August, in the engagement which resulted in Baum's defeat and death. General Stark had command of the American troops in this battle. After the said battle Colonel Simonds' regiment was dismissed, and the deponent returned home.

"The last of August Colonel Simonds was again ordered to take the field with his whole regiment of militia, and was stationed at Pawlet, in Vermont, and subsequently marched, by scouting parties, along the frontier, through Wells and adjoining towns, to Whitehall. The object of this march was to cut off the retreat of stragglers and all communication betwixt the British general, Burgoyne, and Canada. The above campaign continued three and a half months, during which he served as lieutenant in Captain Jude Williams' company of militia, in Colonel Simonds' regiment. Were then dismissed, and returned home to Williamstown in Massachusetts.

"Upon or about the 1st of May, 1778, was appointed lieutenant, to serve in a levy granted by the General Assembly of Massachusetts, in Colonel Wood's regiment, a term of eight months from their arrival in camp. Arrived in camp at Peekskill, in New York, about the 16th of May. Previous to this was occupied, by order, from 1st of May till 16th, in recruiting and marching. Afterwards was occupied most of the ensuing summer at White Plains, New York. Some time in September following, the British army embarked, pursuing their course eastward through the Sound. General Nixon's brigade was dispatched by land to watch their movements. Previously Colonel Wood's regiment had been annexed to General Nixon's brigade. Said Lieutenant Harris marched in this expedition as far as Farmington, in Connecticut,. The British army soon after returning to New York to winter quarters, Wood's regiment was ordered back to Peekskill into winter quarters. Remained there until 1st of February, 1779, when said regiment was dismissed to return home.

"About the middle of May, 1779, was appointed captain of the Second Company of militia, in Colonel Simonds' regiment, and commenced recruiting the next day, by order of Colonel Simonds, to supply deficiencies in the regular army. Was thus employed, with the rank of captain, and in actual service, with command upon the frontiers of Vermont, in the latter part of November, three months."

He also states that he was born in the town of Cornwall, in Litchfield county, in the state of Connecticut, on February 27, 1747. Has lived, since the war of the Revolution, at Rutland, in Vermont, and for the last twenty-five years at Hartford, Washington county, New York.

In the Massachusetts MSS. archives (vol. xix. p. 163.) I find that in 1780, Oct. 12, Capt. Israel Harris with a company of 63 men marched to the northern frontier. They were out eleven days. Their monthly pay was ; Captain £12, Lieut. £8, Sergeant £3, Corporal or Musician £4. Private £2.

In 1782 he took up his residence in Rutland, Vt. His first home was in the east parish and near where its south line joins Clarendon. Afterward

he removed north about half way to the village.
He was one of the original members of the congregational church, organized in 1788, Oct. 5, and
in 1800, Aug. 27, was chosen one of the first
deacons. One of his memories was of hearing
Whitefield preach, probably in Salisbury or Sharon,
Conn., where that evangelist preached in July
1770. (Sedg. p. 42.) In 1784 he was one of the
Rutland select-men. The winter of 1807-8 he spent
with his wife at the house of his son-in-law James
D. Butler, (28) and then removed to south Hartford,
Washington Co., N. Y., where his wife d. in 1833
and he himself in 1836. Mrs. H. told me that she
with other women and their children, on the day
of the battle at Bennington, met to pray in their
log church within sound of the British cannon.
They kept on praying till late at night,—for not
till then did a messenger on horseback come to tell
them that they were safe from the scalping knife.

Samuel Harris (507) m. Hannah Barbara Hufnagel. He d. 1819 or 20. She d. 1849, Dec. 4, in Rutland, Vt.

Their children were :
518. Michael, b. 1777, Feb. 12, Sandy Hill.
519. Rachel[1] ,b. 1778, Aug. 13, Mud St., m. John
      S. Peffier.
520. Christina, b. 1780, June 23, Mud St., m.
      Charles High.
521. Hannah[3] b. 1782, Feb. 14, Cambridge, m.
      John Beebe.

522. Lois[2], b. 1784, Jany. 14, Mud St., m. James D. Butler (28).

523. Samuel[3], b. 1786, June 6, Mud St., m. Ann Griffin.

524. Rosalie[1], b. 1788, Dec. 6, Mud, St., m. Samuel Beebe. She d. 1888, April 29, Elkhart, Ind., in her centennial year,

525. John[7], b. 1792, May 20, Mud St., m. Clara Case.

526. Deborah, b. 1793, Oct. 12, Mud St., m. William Beaumont.

527. Timothy[3], b. 1796, Jany. 28, Mud St., d. Indiana.

528, Charles, b. 1797, May 16, Mud St., d. Kingsbury.

529. Zina, b. 1798, Dec. 2, Mud St.

530. Stephen Van Rensselaer, b. 1801, April 21, Mud St. Alive in 1888.

531. Julia Ann b. 1803, July 25, Mud St. St. d. Kingsbury.

Samuel Harris (507) was b. in the Oblong, Dutchess County, N. Y. His father John Harris (502) was living there in 1751 which was about the time of Samuel's birth. He is said to have been brought up a blacksmith. If so, he probably came with his brother John (504) to the neighborhood of Ft. Ann in 1770.

He appears early in Kingsbury, Washington Co., N. Y. In 1775, Sept. 21, the county recommended him to be commissioned as ensign "he

8

being a friend to the present cause and having
signed the general association", and his commis-
sion was issued the same month by the provincial
congress of New York. More than two years
before, 1773, Feb. 2, his name appears among the
petitioners for selecting Skenesborough as the
county seat. He was married about 1776. His
wife was a daughter of Michael Hufnagel who
came from Frankfort-on-the-Mayn to New York
cit , and once, as the supercargo of a vessel,
returned to his German home. When his daughter
Hannah was born, in 1757, his residence was in the
Bowery, New York, but about ten years after, he
removed to Sandy Hill, where, as a miller, he was
in partnership with Albert Baker. His house, the
second one in the place, was burnt before 1775, and
his family then lived in the same dwelling with the
Bakers. In 1773, Oct. 19, Hufnagel served as a
juryman at the first court held in Fort Edward.
Being a tory, he fled to Canada on the capture of
Burgoyne.

In August, 1777, during Burgoyne's invasion,
Samuel Harris with his wife and one child were
living on Moss St., about a mile north of Sandy
Hill. They would probably have fled the spring
before with his brother John (504) had they not
trusted in the Hufnagel toryism as a protection.
Mrs. H., one day had just taken a batch of biscuit
from the oven, when a party of Indians rushed in,
seized and bound her. They also snatched up her

baby, and wrapped up the biscuit in her cradle-
quilt, and started with the captives and plunder for
the British lines.

Falling in with a Hessian scouting-party, she
appealed to them in their own German so movingly
that they drew their swords and put the Indians to
flight. They thus released the captives, but could
not save either the biscuit or the baby-blanket.
In 1782, at the organization of the town, he was
chosen town-clerk, and held the office for a dozen
years. As to religion he was a Moravian. A
Moravian mission house was built on the west bank
of Indian Pond a little south of the Oblong, about
the year 1740. A marble monument of the Mova-
rian mission was erected here in 1859. His brother
Jonathan is mentioned in 1789 as Lieutenant, and
Captain in 1796. Though the name Jonathan does
not appear in the list in this work as a brother of
Samuel, such a brother may well have been among
the younger children of John Harris, born where
there was no public record of births.

Samuel Harris was the town-clerk of Kingsbury,
in 1782, also in 1784 and every year following
until 1794 inclusive.*

His last sickness was a cancer in the eye.
The original of his *Will*, a long and curious docu-
ment, is in the hands of his grandson John K.
Harris. (612)

---

* See Gazetteer of Washington Co., 1849-50.

SEVENTH GENERATION

John Harris (508) m. 1801, Feb. 19, Elizabeth Bingham. He d. 1828, May 23, Centerville, O. She d 1845, Feb. 11. Their children all except Laura, b. in Montgomery Co., O., were :

> 548. Laura[1] b. 1801, Nov. 19, 1820, Oct. 5, m. Reuben Munger. She d. 1875, July 9.
>
> 549. John[2] b. 1803, Dec. 5 ; 1826 Oct. 30, m. Lucinda Mitchell. He d. 1849.
>
> 550. Alvan B., b. 1807, Feb. 5, d. unmarried 1839, Sept. 8.
>
> 551. Sarah[1], b. 1809, May 3, m. 1827, Oct. 2, Festus E. Munger. She d. 1864, Feb. 4.
>
> 552. Samuel[1], b. 1811, Dec. 28. He d. 1839, Feb. 17.
>
> 553. James B., b. 1814, Feb. 7, m. Julia A. Briar. He d. 1856, Mar. 10.

Twins   (Porter, b. 1816. He died 1834.
554.   {   Perry, b. 1816, April 9, m. Laura B. Harris (584). He died 1843.
555.   (ris (584). He died 1843.

> 556. William[1], b. 1819, March 30, 1847, Feb. 11, m. Eusebia Blodget. He d. 1851, Nov. 11.
>
> 557. Elizabeth[7], b. 1820, Dec. 8, d. unmarried 1879, Mar. 22.

John Harris (508) came to Ohio from Vermont in 1797, and first settled in Zanesville. From there, in 1801, he removed with his brother Israel to Centerville. His journey was in February, and lasted seventeen days. Thirteen nights he camped out. He is described as tall, thin and of dark complexion. ·

Elizabeth Harris (509), 1791, Dec. 1, m. William McConnell, b. 1767. She d. 1817, Dec. 12, Hartford, N. Y. He d. 1850, May 10, Rutland, Vt.

Their children were b. there, namely :

558. Israel, b. 1795, d. Oconomowoc, Wis., 1871.

559. Thomas, b. 1797, d. Girard, Pa., 1840.

560. Elizabeth², b. 1801, d. Hartford, N. Y., 1877.

561. Henry, b. 1804, d. Girard, Pa., 1871.

562. Almira, b. 1807, d. Brooklyn, Ia., 1872.

563. William, b. 1812, lives Georgetown, Cal.

564. Chloe, b. 1815, d. Hinsdale, N. H., 1860.

The above children were all b. in Rutland, Vt.

Sarah Harris (510) m. Benjamin Wooster. She d. 1824, Oct. 19. He d. 1840, Feb. 18.

Their children were :

565. Sarah Harris, b. 1799, March 6, in Cornwall, Vt.

566. Benjamin Harris Restored, b. 1811, in Fairfield, Vt.

567. Charlotte Eliza, b. 1813, Fairfield, Vt.

568. Louisa Cornelia, b. 1815, Fairfield, Vt.

Rachel Harris (511) m. James D. Butler (28).

Israel Harris (512) m Betsey Mead. He d. 1855, March 22, in Centreville, O.

Their children were :

569. James[2], b. 1801, March 31.

570. Abner, b. 1803, Dec. 23.

For second wife m. Elizabeth McCann, b. 1783.

Their children were :

563 bis. Rachel[5], b. 1815, Aug. 17, m. Nat. Sunderland.

564 bis. Elizabeth[2], b. 1817.

565 bis. Nancy, b. 1821, March 14, m. Frank Larew.

566 bis. Mary[3], b. 1825, March 27, m. ——— Furrow.

567 bis. Sarah[6], b. 1828, March 1, m. Dr. G. Winfield Stipp, Bloomington, Ill.

568 bis. Israel[4], b. 1829, lives Chicago, Ill., 1888.

569 bis. Ellen, b. 1832, March 30, m. W. Packard.

570 bis. Rachel, m. ——— Sunderland, lives Learned, Kansas. Her dau. m. ——— McClure.

571 bis. Elizabeth, Bloomington, Ill.

Samuel Harris (513) 1809, Feb. 26, m. Relief Noble, b. Tinmouth. He d. 1871, June 11. She d. 1878.

Their children were :

571. Lois Noble, b. 1811, Jan. 16.

572. Samuel Noble, b. 1812, Dec. 14, m. 1836, April 26, Abigail Marie Stone.

573. Susan Willard, b. 1818, March 1, m. 1837,
. Jan. 1, George Coulter.

574. Laura Eliza, b. 1823, Oct 1, m. 1850, March
5, Manuel McDonald.

Joseph Harris (514) m. Lucretia Lord. He d.
1830, July 13, Hartford, N. Y. She d. Romeo,
Mich., 1866, Nov. 23.

Their children were :

575. Joseph L.,⁵ b. 1806, Feb. 7.

576. Lucretia, b. 1808, Jan. 24.

577. Louisa, b. 1810, April 10.

578. Laura², b. 1812, Aug. 26.

579. Lydia Ann, b. 1814, June 19.

580. James³, b. 1817, March 24.

581. Mary¹, b. 1819, Aug. 26.

582. George, b. 1822.

James Harris² (580) d. Des Moines, 1857, Nov. 4.
His wife Cornelia Wedder, d. next day. No children.

Timothy Harris (515) m. Bethiah Linnel. He d.
1822, March 28. She was b. 1790, April 19 in Mass.,
d. 1873, July 28. Her 80th birth-day was celebrated
by a gathering of many descendants.

Their children were :

583. Chloe Lucretia, b. 1810, May 29.

584. Laura Bethiah, b. 1812, May 23.

585. Harriet Newell, b. 1815, Nov. 19.

586. Sarah Knowles, b. 1818, May 28.

587. Mary⁵, d. an infant.

The widow of Timothy Harris (515) m. in 1823, John B. Cooley, M. D.

Their children were :

588. Loanna Zeruiah, b. 1824, Aug. 26.
589. Timothy Harris, b. 1827, April 9.
590. Emma Barber.
591. Georgiana Barber, b. 1832, Oct. 5.

Lois Harris (516) m. Obadiah Noble, b. 1777, Feb. 13. She d. 1809. He d. 1864, March 1.

Their only child was :

592. Jonathan Harris, b. 1804, Oct. 8, in Tinmouth, Vt. He m. Octavia Porter, b. Tinmouth, Vt., 1804, Jan. 23, d. 1865, Oct. 17. In 1866, Nov. 13, he m. Caroline M. Chamberlain in Aurora, Ill. Graduated at Williams College, 1826, Presbyterian pastor in Carbondale, Pa., and Schaghticoke, N. Y., and D. D.

[NOTES.]

Wm. McConnell, father of 558 et seqq., was of the Scotch Irish race who settled Londonderry, N. H., 1718. His father Thomas, b. 1729, was said to have been a member of the Boston Tea-party. He settled in Rutland about 1778. Died there 1789 March 18.

Benjamin Wooster, father of 565 et seqq., b. in Waterbury, Conn., 1767, Oct, 29, was pastor of the Congregational church in Fairfield, Vt., from 1804.

40. He was opposed to the war of 1812. but in 1814, when the British came up Lake Champlain, and when he was well-nigh fifty years old, he headed a company of volunteers, and marched for Plattsburg on the very day he was to preach a preparatory lecture. For this patriotism Gov. Tompkins of New York, sent him a magnificent bible with a letter written on the fly-leaf which was published in Niles *Register* (Vol. VIII. pp. 309, 318.) A biographical sermon concerning him by Rev. A. W. Wild, has been published. He was of gigantic stature. as well as great wit and readiness at repartee.

Samuel Harris, father of 571 et seqq., in boyhood at Rutland, had his skull broken by the kick of a horse so that it needed to be trepanned. In 1819, Sept. 5, he was on board the steamer *Phœnix*, which was then burned between Burlington and Plattsburg. Eight lives were lost, and he was on a floating plank from midnight till dawn. He stood close by a man killed in Rutland by the bursting of a cannon. Nor were these all his hair-breadth escapes, yet he survived all his nine brothers and sisters.

Timothy Harris (515) father of 583 et seqq., b. 1781, d. 1822. From 1798 to 1801 was fitted for college in Cornwall, Vt , by his brother-in-law Rev. Benjamin Worcester, see (565). He was graduated at Middlebury College in 1805. In 1803 he taught for three months in Holden, Mass. He was led to visit the west, it would seem, by the fact that his brothers John and Israel were Ohio pioneers, as well as by hopes that the climate would improve his health.

In July 1853, I copied the following words from his tombstone in Granville, Ohio ; " Rev. Timothy Harris was born in Williamstown, Mass., March 15, 1781 ; graduated at Middlebury College, August 21, 1805 ; licensed to preach the gospel May 27, 1807 ; ordained and installed the first pastor of the Congregational church in Granville, Ohio, Dec. 14, 1808. He died beloved and lamented, March 28, 1822. During his ministry of fourteen years one hundred and fifty united with the church. Well done good and faithful servant ! " The text of his installation sermon, I Timothy, vi : 20, was repeated to me seventy years afterward by one Avery who had heard it.

His study of divinity was in Rupert, Vt., with Rev. Mr. Preston. After removing to Ohio he made only one visit to the East. This visit occupied well-nigh a year from October 1813, till August 1814. His wife and daughter Laura, then under two years old, went with him. Mrs. H. was taken sick in Mantua soon after starting. After two weeks she seemed able to travel, but the fall mud had become so deep that they were obliged to wait for sleighing. Spring mud set in before they had run through their round of eastern visits.

Michael Harris (518) m. Susan Allen, b. 1779, who was of English birth. He d. 1820 Sept. 13, at Warrensburg, N. Y. Buried at Moss St.

Their children were :

593. Leonard G., b. 1813, Nov. 8, Caldwell, N. Y. m. Rosalie (605). See 688.

594. George Samuel, b. 1815, March 22, Caldwell, N. Y., m. Sarah Bacon (121). See 227.

595. Michael.

596. James.[1]

597. Frederick.

Christina Harris (520) m. Charles High. She d. 1841, Aug. 11.

Among their children were :

598. Charles[2], b. 1812.

599. Maria, b. 1798, April 14, m. 1822, July 13, Samuel Allen, brother of Michael's (518) wife.

Hannah Harris (521) m. John Beebe.

Their children were :

600. Ann, m. Joseph L. Harris (575). See 645.

601. George.

602. Henry.

Nos. 601 and 602, were blind from birth. They lived to manhood, and d. at a blind asylum in New York city.

Samuel Harris (523) m. Ann Griffin. He d. 1842, May 7, at Elkhart, Ind.

Their children were :

603. Thomas G., b. 1817, April 8.

604. Hannah⁴,b. 1819.

605. Rosalie, b. 1821, June 14, m. Leonard G. (593).

606. Edgar, b. ———, d. 1886, in Hancock, Potta-watomee Co,, Iowa.

607. Samuel⁵, b. 1830 ca , d. California.

608. Charles, d. California.

Hannah (604) m. Rev. S. D. Smith, Lithopolis, O.

Their children were Charles and Henry b. 1844. Charles is a druggist, Hillsdale, Mich.

Rosalie Harris (524) m. Samuel Beebe.

Their children were :

John Harris (525) m. Clarinda S. Case, in Ticon-deroga, N. Y. She was b. 1796. He d. 1876, Dec. 14, Floyd C. H., Va. She d. Harrodsburg, Ky., 1871, April 7.

Their only child was :

612. John Kellogg, b. 1832, Feb. 16.

Deborah Harris (526) m. Wm. Beaumont.

John Harris (612) and (638 bis.) graduated at Williams College 1852 ; Union Seminary, N. Y., 1858 ; 1852-54, teacher at National School of Choctaws, Indian Ter. Presbyterian preacher, Amherst, Rockbridge Co., Va., 1858-68: 1868-71, Head of Harrodsburg Female College ; preacher in Nebraska, 1872-4, Red Cloud, then in Scotia, Greely Co.

EIGHTH GENERATION.

Laura Harris (548) b. 1820, Oct. 5. m. Reuben Munger. She d. 1875, July 9.

Their children were :

620. Edmund H., b. 1821.
621. John Eno, b. 1827.
622. Amanda, b 1829.

Sarah Harris (551) m. Festus E. Munger.

Their children were :

623. Harris, b. 1828, Sept. 12, m. 1850, July 31, E. Cartwright.
624. Eunice, b. 1831, Feb. 24, d. at four years.
625. Felix, b. 1833, Dec. 1, m. 1865, Nov. 26, Sarah Adams,
626. Timothy, b. 1838, Feb. 11, m. 1865, March 9, C. Brennan.
627. Lyman. b. 1842, Aug. 22, m. 1864, March 1, M. Reynolds.
628. Alvan, b. 1845, June 6.
629. Laura Eliza, b. 1848, Dec. 27, m. John W. Hayes.

James Harris (569) m. Rebecca Jennings, b. 1804, Oct. 3.

Their children were :

623 bis. Israel Hopkins, b. 1823, Nov. 23.
624 bis. Joseph, b 1827.
625 bis. Alfred Jennings, b. 1834, May 3.

Abner Harris (570) m. 1826, Oct. 26, Susan Watkins. b. 1806, d. 1882, m. 1885, Oct. 22, Hattie Oberchain, of Ky., b. 1851, Aug. 6.

John Harris[6] (549), 1826, Oct. 30, m. Lucinda Mitchell. He d. 1848.

Their children were :

620 bis. Cornelia, b. 1828, April 11, d. young.

621 bis. Eliza, b. 1830, Sept. 12, d. 1850.

622 bis. William[5], b. 1833, March 14, m. 1854, April 7.

623 bis. John Porter, b. 1835, March 31, m. 1862, Nov. 27.

624 bis. Margaret, b. 1837, Dec. 8, m. 1856, Sept. 5.

625 bis. Edward, b. 1839, Sept. 15, m. 1859, Jan. 5.

626 bis. Laura E., b. 1842, June 27, d. ———.

627 bis. Henry Clay, b. 1844, May 14, m. 1866, Oct. 28.

628 bis. Reuben Munger, b. 1847, Oct. 17, m. 1867, March 1.

Israel McConnell (558) m. Vesta Brown.

Their children were :

630. Horace, d. cholera, 1849, Jefferson City.

631. Edward, drowned 1860.

632. Albert.

633. Louisa.

634. Rosamond.

Thomas McConnell (559). 1821, Jan. 6, m. his cousin Margaret McConnell. He d. 1840, May 1, in Girard, Pa.

Their children who grew up :

635. Delia, b. 1821. Oct. 31, m. Cyrus Dickson.
636. George Thomas, b. 1825.
637. J. Julius, b. 1827.

Elizabeth McConnell (560) m. Sheldon Spring.

Henry McConnell (561) m. Charlotte Webster Townsend.

Their only child was :

638. Rebecca, m. Dan Rice, had son of same name.

Almira McConnell (562) m. George S. Stewart.

639. William Le Roy, b. Rutland, Vt., 1834, April 19, lives Whitewater, Wis.
640. Francis Edgar.
641. Henry Thomas.
642. Mary Elizabeth.

Chloe McConnell (564) m. Henry Packer. She d. 1860, Hinsdale, N. H.

Their children were :

643. Delia Elizabeth, b. 1854.
644. Ella Gertrude, m.——— Kernshaw of Grand Island.

John K. Harris (612) m. Chloe Minerva Bigelow. She was b. 1830, Dover, Vt.

Their children were :

638 bis. Clara E., b. 1860, March 27, Rockbridge Co., Va.
639 bis. John L., b. 1867, June 17, Amherst C. H., Va.

640 bis. Susan Maria, b. 1869, Feb. 7. Amherst, C. H., Va.

641 bis. Mary Adelaide, b. 1871, March 27, Christiansburg, Va.

642 bis. James Ramsey, b. 1872, Harrodsburg, Ky., d. an infant.

Joseph L. Harris (575) m. Ann Beebe (545). Their children were :

645. Josephine Lucretia, b. 1833, Dec. 6, m. Van Ness Pierce. She d. 1888, Jan. 19 in Englewood, Ill.

646. Kate Mary, b. 1835, Oct. 3.

647. Charles Gerald, b. 1837, Jan. 10.

Lucretia Harris (576) m. Jacob Holmes. Their children were :

648. George Henry, d. Milwaukee, 1883, Jan.

649. Richard S., b. 1842, July 6, Brooklyn, N. Y.

650. Clara, m. Cyrus G Knowles, San José.

651. Emma. m. Henry H. Rhodes, San José.

652. Anna, m. Rev. Geo. William Knox, missionary in Japan, has three children.

Louisa Harris (577) m. George Chandler, b. Granville, N. Y., 1800, May 16, d. Romeo, Mich., 1867, Feb. 18. She d. Flint, Mich., 1886, Nov. 2, buried in Romeo. Their children were :

653. France, b. 1834, Feb. 13.

654. William, b. 1836, Jan. 11.

655. Edward Bruce, b. 1838, Jan. 30

656. Marion Lord, b. 1840, April 6.

657. Isabella, b. 1842, May 21.

658. Louisa Amy, b. 1844, Oct. 20.

Nos. 653, 654 graduated at Ann Arbor in 1854.
No. 655 in 1858.

William McConnell (563) m. Hannah L. Braddish.
She was b. 1821, July 11, at Elk Creek, Pa. They
were m. there.

Their children were :

645 bis. Margaret E., b. 1849, May 15, Whitewater, Wis.

646 bis. Mary B., b. 1856, March 5, Georgetown,
Cal.

647 bis. Frank W., b. 1857, May 23, Georgetown,
Cal.

Wm. McConnell (563) removed early from Vermont to West Bloomfield, Ontario Co., N. Y., to
Rushville, Schuyler Co., Ill., to Platea and Girard,
Pa., to Hanover, Columbiana Co., O., to Whitewater, Wis.

In 1849 he went overland to California by Cooke's
route, through New Mexico and Arizona to Los
Angeles. Thence he sailed for San Francisco and
arrived there Dec. 6, 1849. Settling in Georgetown in 1854 he has remained there ever since, save
three years from 1864-67 in Pennsylvania.

Laura Harris (578) m. 1833, Ebenezer Lord.

Their children were :

659. Fanny E., b. 1855, Sept. 4.

660. William, b. ———, d. 1865, April, Columbus, O.

9

The second husband of Laura Harris (578) was Bliss Shaw, m. in 1844.

Their children were :

661. Laura C., m. Elisha Chapin.

662. Lydia, m. Wm. H. Platt.

Lydia Ann Harris (579) m. 1835, Feb. 22, John C. Bishop, b. 1813, Jan. 23. Resides Granville Corners, N. Y. He d. 1879, Aug. 16, Granville.

Their children were :

662 bis. Isaac, b. 1836, May 31.

663. Laura, b. 1838, Sept. 10.

663 bis. Anna M., b. 1841, Nov. 2, d. 1842, May 31.

664. Antoinette Agan, b. 1843, Oct. 31.

665. Lucy Myers, b. 1850, Dec. 17.

Mary Harris (580) m. Richard Sill. She d. 1864, Sept. 25, in Romeo. He d. 1845.

Their only child was :

666. Helen, b. 1841, m. Samuel A. Read.

George Harris (581) m. Sarah Field.

Their children were :

667. Fanny Loraine, b. 1850, July 6, Glens Falls.

668. Minnie Field, b. 1853, Feb. 12, Plattsburg.

669. Charles Salter, b. ———, Minneapolis.

Chloe L. Harris (583) m. Rev. Timothy Howe.

Their golden wedding 1883, Nov. 9, was celebrated at Pataskala where Mr. Howe had been Presbyterian pastor from 1838 to '76.

Their children were :

670. Brainard H , b. 1839.

671. Archer Perkins, b. 1842.

672. Sarah Melissa, b. 1847.

673. Timothy Butler, b. 1853.

Laura B. Harris (584) 1838, Sept. 10, m. Perry Harris (556).

Their only child was :

674. Clarissa Dell, m. Roderick Stevens. Laura's second husband was Elymas Wheaton.

One of their children was :

675. Timothy Harris.

Harriet N. Harris (585) m. James L. Mitchell.

Their children were :

676. Frances, b. 1838, m. Isaac Williams.

677. Quincy, b. 1841.

678. Newell, b. 1844, m. Henrietta Melschuer.

679. William, b. 1849.

680. Ella Butler, b. 1853.

681. Clara Louise, b. 1856. Teacher of imbeciles, Columbus, O.

Sarah K. Harris (586) m. Henry P. Smythe.

Their children were :

682. Emma B., b. 1845, June 9.

683. Myra Bosworth, b. 1848, Sept. 13.

684. Arthur Harris, b. 1850, Nov. 14.

685. Henry Herbert, b. 1854, July 12.

686. Perry Parmele, b. 1857, Oct. 21.

687. Edmund Worth, b. 1861, Sept. 30, d. 1864, Aug. 15.

No. 685 graduated at Kenyon college, is Episcopal rector at North Adams, Mass.

Leonard G. Harris (593) m. Rosalie Harris (605) 1842, May 23, Pleasant Plain, Elkhart Co., Ind He d. 1853, Nov. 14, South Bend.

Their children were :

688. Charles Butler, b. 1843, m. 1869, Oct. 18, Julia E. Latta, Goshen, Ind.

689. Sarah Rosalie[3], d. 1888, Feb 11, m. May 1, 1866, Nat. P. Jacobs.

690. Mary Eliza[6], b. 1848, May 7, m. 1870, May 17, John A. Roach.

The second husband of Rosalie (605) m. 1858, Aug. 19, at Goshen, Ind., was Dr. E. W. H. Ellis. He d. 1876, Oct.

George S. Harris (594) m. Sarah Bacon (121). (See No. 227).

Thomas G. Harris (603) m. 1846, Dec. 17, at Niles, Mich., Maria McLure, b. Townsend, Vt., 1831, March 5. He d. 1859, Feb. 9, Goshen, Ind. She d. 1886, July 30, Minneapolis.

Their children were :

691. Samuel Arthur, b. 1847, Oct. 25.

692. Katharine, b. 1855, Dec. 22.

Sarah H. Wooster (565) 1817, Oct. 15, m. Harmon
 . Northup. She d. 1882.

Their children were :

Joseph, lives in St. Albans.

Wooster, lives in Fairfield.

Julian, lives in Fairfield.

Charlotte, lives in Sheldon, m. —— Deming.

Charlotte E. Wooster (567] m. Hezekiah Com-
stock. She lives in Shelburne, Vt., is now, 1888, a
widow, and has lost all her five children.

Samuel N. Harris (572) 1836, April 26, m. Abigail
Marie Stone.

Their children were :

554 bis. Elizabeth, m. ——— Styles.

555 bis. Ida, m. ——— Keeler.

556 bis. Adeline, m. ——— Willis.

557 bis. Roderick.

558 bis. William.

Maria High (599) 1822, July 13, m. Samuel Allen.
He was b. Gloucester, Eng., 1789, June 30. She d.
1880, June 11.

Among their children were :

Charles.

George R., b. 1838, June 30, Kingsbury,
N. Y.

William.

Samuel Allen was brought up in Caldwell, N. Y.,
removed to Indiana in 1839, and to Wisconsin in

1841, settling in Bloomfield, Walworth Co. His sister Susan m. Michael Harris (518) and after his death John Wilson.

NINTH GENERATION.

Mary E. Harris (690) m. John A. Roach.
Their children were :
684 bis. Robert H , b. 1870, Dec.
685 bis. Leonard H., b. 1872, Dec.
686 bis. Charles H., b. 1876, Dec.
687 bis. Rosalie II., b. 1881, May.
688 bis. Walter Oatman, b. 1884, Oct.
Edmund H. Munger (620) 1861, Oct. 3, m. Emily
    A. Mather.
Their children were :
700. Clara, b. 1862, July 13, m. Rev. Joseph A.
    Littell, Albany, N. Y.
701. John, b. 1863, Dec. 24.
702. Laura Eliza, b. 1866, Oct. 28.
703. Edmund, b. 1869, Sept. 26.
704. Mary Augusta, b, 1871, Oct. 15.
705, Charles Mather, b. 1876, April 13.
Delia McConnell (635) m. Cyrus Dickson.
Their children were :
706. Maggie, b. 1841, Jan. 19.
707. Eva Reynolds, b. 1843, m. W. W. Smith,
    Nebraska City.

708. Fanny Delia, b. 1845, m. Frank J. Leavens, Norwich, Conn.

Richard Holmes (649) 1869, Oct. 20, m. Fannie P. Olmstead, in Auburn, N. Y She d. 1878, Dec. 9. His wife Alida L. Dodge, was m. 1881, Sept. 7 in Newburgh, N. Y. Their dau. Mabel D., b. 1883, Jan. 9.

Their children were : Edith C., b 1871, March 16, Carrol O., b. 1874, April 16. He was graduated Middlebury. 1862 and became pres pastor Nov. 1. 1887, in Warren, Pa.

William Chandler (654) 1863, Sept. 22, m. Lizzie Boyden. He d. 1868, Oct. 11. He enlisted in Chicago Light Artillery, in 1861 ; was in various actions and became a Lieut., in Waterhouse's Battery.

E. B. Chandler (655) 1872, Jan. 9, m. Emily Moseley, of Princeton, Ill.

Their children were :

712. Alice, b. 1872, Oct. 11.

713. George Moseley, b. 1876, March 27.

George B. Harris (228) m. Mary Rose Hunt, b. 1849, Mount Morris, N. Y., dau. of Sanford Hunt, who m. Marilla Currier.

John Lawton m. Fanny L. Harris (667) at San Francisco, July 24, '72.

Their children were :

401 bis. Elizabeth, b. June 13, 1873.

402 bis. Loraine Harris, b. Dec. 25, 1874.

403 bis. Fannie, b. July 25, 1878.

404 bis. John, b. Feb. 14, 1881.

405 bis. Kenneth A., b. Jan. 2. 1883.

406 bis. Howard Mills, b. May 23, 1884.

Alonzo K. Hollis m. Minnie F. Harris (668) at San Francisco, Feb. 12, 1873.

Their children were :

407 bis. Nellie Lord, b. Dec. 2 1873.

408 bis. Georgia Harris, b. Oct. 1, 1875.

409 bis. Arthur Garfield, b. June 30, 1830.

Isabella Chandler (657) m. T. D. Simonton.

Their children were :

714. Alfred Bruce, d. early

715. Annie, d. early.

716. William, d. early.

717. Helen, d. early.

718. James Carlyle, b. ———

Louisa Amy Chandler (658) 1868, June, m. Frank C. Begole.

Their only child who grew up was :

719. Josiah W.

Her second husband was W. C. Green, m. 1880, March 17, in Chicago.

Fanny E. Lord (659) 1855, Sept. 4, m. John Bliss, b. 1831, Sept. 28, Canaan, N. Y. (See *Bliss Genealogy*, p. 36, No. 3440, etc.)

Their children were :

720. John Lord, b. 1856, Oct. 21.

720 bis. George Lathrop, b. 1859, Dec. 27, d. 1861 Aug. 2.

721. Fanny Louise, b. 1862, July 7.

721 bis. Frank Harris, b. 1864, Aug. 4, d. 1865, Sept. 16.

722. William Lord, b. 1871, July 16.

722 bis. Edith Fowler, b. 1868, Aug. 9, d. 1870, Aug. 14.

723. Edith Mary, b. 1875. Feb. 18.

John Bliss was namesake of his father, who was b. in 1795, and in 1830 m. Abby Williams.

Laura Catharine Shaw (661) May 5, 1870. m. Elisha Sterling Chapin, 414 Quincy St., Brooklyn.

Their children were :

723 bis. Elisha Sterling, b. 1884. Feb. 29.

724. Henry Sterling, b. 1871, Feb. 15.

724 bis. Lida Frances, b. Sept. 8, 1885.

725. Laura Harris, b. 1875, July 29.

Laura Bishop (663) m. George Tobey.

Their children were :

726 bis. Edith Lord, b. 1867, April 21.

727 bis. Edward Azro, b. 1870, June 7.

728 bis. Herbert Bishop, b. 1871, May 2.

729 bis. Antoinette Louise, b. 1878, Aug. 26.

Antoinette A. Bishop (664) m. Deliverance Rogers.

Their dau. was : Flora Antoinette, b. 1866, Aug. 31.

Lucy M. Bishop (665) m. 1871, Dec. 28, George Washington Henry.

Their children were :

Harry, b. 1873, Nov. 22, d. 1874, July 1.

Helen Eliza, b. 1879, Dec. 4.

Celia E. Harris (227) 1883, July 25, m. Nathan S. Harwood, of Lincoln Neb.

Their children are .

721 bis. Agnes, b. 1884, April 12, d. 14 April.

722 bis. George Harris, b. 1885, Aug. 10, d. 1887, Feb. 10.

723 bis. Anne Dorrance, b. 1887, April 6.

Arthur H. Smythe (684) m. Grace A. Parmele, 1876, Oct 11, Greenbush, N. Y.

Their children are :

726. Bessie Harris, b. 1877, June 29.

727. Arthur Irwin, b. 1880, July 14.

728. Alice Ring, b. 1882, Aug. 26.

729. Burdette Randall, b. 1884, Nov. 18.

Emma B. Smythe (682) m. Calvin H. Reed,) of Toledo, O.

Their children are :

730. Morgan Smythe, b. 1872, Feb. 20.

731. Harris Hamilton, b. 1873, Nov. 3, d. 1879, Aug. 14.

732. Chase Campbell, b. 1875, Feb. 6.

733. Carl Kirkley, b. 1876, July 15, d. 1882, Oct. 24.

734. Linnel Lecky, b. 1877, Aug. 17.

Henry H. Smythe (685) 1882, July 12, m. L. Charlotte Wilbor.

Their children are :

Perry P. Smythe (686) 1882, March 9, m. Nellie McColm.

Their children are :

Frederick L. Harris (232) in 1882, June 20, m. Jessie E. Mason.

Their children are :

735. Mary Turner, b. 1883, July 17, Lincoln.

735 bis. Fred Mason, b. in Ord., Neb., 1885, Oct. 2,

730 bis. Sarah Butler, b. Ord., Neb., 1887, Nov. 4.

Edward Kirk Harris (233) m. Hattie Turner.

Children :

731 bis. Clara Funke, b. in Ord., Neb., 1886. Dec. 26.

Margaret E. McConnell (645 bis.) m. J. C. Coffman. Residence Platea, Erie Co., Pa.

Their children are Perry J. and Carrie F.

Israel H. Harris (623 bis) 1848. Nov. 8, m. Hester Ann Stokes.

Their daughter was :

736. Caroline Emma.

Charles L. Harris (230) m. 1883, Jan. 17, Mary E.
Day in Shelbyville, Ind.

Their child :

737. Celia Ellen, b. 1885, Sept. 13, Neligh, Neb.

Samuel A. Harris (691) 1872, Sept. 16, m. Anna
Catharine Stewart.

Their children are :

737. Walter Stewart, b. 1874, Feb. 13.

738. Katharine McClure, b. 1881, Oct. 30.

739. Thomas Stewart, b. 1883, Oct. 1.

Edward K. Harris (233) 1885, Oct. 28, m. Hattie
Funke.

Brainard H. Howe (670) m. Sarah A. Beecher.
Their children were :

741. Mary, b. 1866, July.

742. Jennie, b. 1868, Nov.

743. Edward, b. 1875, Aug.

Sarah M. Howe (672) m Ralph Burnett Pierson.
Their children were :

744. Marietta Harris, b 1868.

745 Loanna Howe, b. 1870.

746 Edna Harrington. b. 1871

747. Archer Dudley, b. 1873.

748. Lora, b. 1875.

749. Charles Bertram, b. 1876.

742 bis. Ernest, b. 1878.

743 bis. Davie, b 1880.

744 bis. Samuel, b. 1883.

Clara E. Harris (638 bis) m. 1885, Dec. 25, Prof. J. T. Akers, Central Univ., Ky.

Their children are :

741 bis. Arthur Akers, b. 1886, Nov. 6, Richmond, Ky. ˙˙ .

TENTH GENERATION.

Eva R. Dickson (707) m. W. W. Smith.

Their children are :

751. Fanny Dickson, b. 1869, May 5.

752. Evelyn Wilson, b. 1876, Sept. 8.

Frances D. Dickson (708) m. Frank J. Leavens.

Their children were :

753. Eva Dickson, b. 1876, Jan. 26, d. ——

754. Faith Robinson, b. 1877, April 11.

755. Delia Dickson, b. 1878, Sept 14.

756. Dickson, b. 1887.

John Lord Bliss (720) 1879, Dec. 4, m. Elizabeth McArthur Hutchison, b. 1858, May 16, Brooklyn. Her parents were from Glasgow, Scotland.

Their children are :

Elizabeth, b. 1887, May 9. She d. 1888, May 4.

A RACIAL CHARACTERISTIC.

Both the Butler and the Harris families have shown a proneness for pioneering. Both landed in Massachusetts in the first decade of its existence

The Butlers settled on the Kennebec before the opening of the Revolution—and before its close had established thamselves 60 miles inland from Boston. In the next decade three of them were living in Vermont, then deemed the far northwest. One of them had made his home west of the Mississippi before 1810, and before 1820 another was plowing west of Cincinnati.

The Harris race is still more fond of the backwoods. In the third decade after the founding of Boston some of them broke up land west of the Connecticut, and as settlement spread westward they were always leading its van. Thus they entered New York, pushed up the Hudson, lingered a little among the Green Mountains but had planted themselves in Ohio before the year 1800. They scattered into Indiana, Illinois, Michigan, Wisconsin, Missouri, Nebraska, California. One of them was long ago a missionary in Japan.

Stepping westward seems to be,
A kind of Harris destiny.

SIGOURNEY LINEAGE.

James Butler (25) m. Mary Sigourney. (822)

801. Andrew Sigourney, the first of the name known to me, was born in France about the year 1643. He spelled his name André Cigournai, and was a Huguenot.

In 1681 he fled from Rochfort in western France, a port on the Charente about seven miles from its mouth, which is near the city of Rochelle. His wife, born Charlotte Pairan, fled with him. They took with them their four children :

802. Susan.

803. Peter.

804. Charlotte

805. Andrew, as well as his nephew Alexander Cigournai. At all events these persons were with him the next spring in London.

In the French National Archives, at the Paris In-
tendant's office, his name appears in the list of fugitives from Rochfort, with the note *point de bien*, (T.
T. No. 254) that is, leaving nothing to be confiscated.
It has been hence conjectured that he merely came
to Rochfort to embark, and that his home was at
some place in the interior. There is some ground
for believing that place to have been Saint Jean
d'Angely, which lies inland a few miles east of
Rochfort.

From that Angely many Huguenots fled, one of
them was Esaie Sigourney and his wife who in
1708 are mentioned in the register of Rider's Court
French church, St. Ann's, Westminster. (Agnew
III, p. 36.) In the same town there was then a
Huguenot, Peter Sigourney [Pierre Sigournet]
who was a *Maistre Cordonnier*, a master shoemaker. But Andrew of whom I am writing was a
Huguenot and a shoemaker. He also named his
oldest son Peter. It hence seems to me not unlikely
that Andrew was a kinsman of Peter, and that he
lived in the same town of Angely.

In 1682 Andrew Sigourney with his wife, four
children and nephew before-mentioned, was naturalized in Westminster. (Agnew, III, p. 36.) On
April 16th of the same year, his son Bartholomew
was baptized in the French church in Threadneedle
street, London. The sponsors were Bartholomew
(in honor of whom the boy's name seems to have
been given), Morin and Anne de Granger. Morin

was naturalized with Andrew Sigourney. The registers are in Somerset House, London.

Andrew Sigourney (805) m. Mary Germaine born about 1684, and a John Germaine was naturalized at London in 1688, Aug. 16. (Agnew III, p. 50.) This was no doubt Jean Germon who appears among the fugitives from La Tremblade which is a town not far from Rochfort on the river Seudre, and five miles from the sea.

Andrew Sigourney (801) in 1693 described himself as about fifty years of age. If so, he was born about 1643.

The first vessel bringing Huguenot passengers arrived in Boston in 1686, about the first of July. She came by way of Saint Christopher. This island 17° 17′, was settled by French and English who both arrived on the same day, in 1625. Its chief export was sugar. Twelve of the French and their physician had died on the passage. There were fifteen families, and the survivors in them numbered more than eighty. As they were in great destitution, contributions were taken up for them in the churches. Among those who died at sea, as family tradition has it, was the mother of Mary Germaine, then an infant not yet a year old and who grew up to become the wife of Andrew Sigourney. (806)

Dr. Baird, in his work on the Huguenots, sets down Andrew Sigourney as from a hamlet named Sigournais, of 800 souls in La Vendee, but in cor

10

respondence he fell in with the Angely origin
which I have given, and the suggestion of which I
owe to a Parisian periodical analogous to the
London Notes and Queries, namely, *L'Interme-
diaire*, Vol. xix, p. 688. In the French archives
concerning Rochfort in the *Liste des familles de la
religion pretendue reformée* we find :

    1. *noms et surnoms*, André Sejournay.

    2. *Qualites ou professions*, cordonnier.

    3. *Femmes et enfants*, sa femme et un enfant.

[The other three children may have been carried
out secretly, or remained unnoticed by accident.
All children over a certain age were detained to be
brought up as Catholics.]

    4. *valeur de leur biens*, point de bien.

    5. *année de leur depart*, 1681.

    6. *Lieux de leur retraite*, Angleterre.

It is an old family tradition that the Sigourneys,
having soldiers billeted in their house, made them
a feast and while the intruding guests caroused,
escaped them and reached a vessel which bore
them to England.

It is thought that some French settlers came to
Oxford in 1686. In the next year 52 persons had
established themselves there. In 1694 a mill had
been built. The chief promoter of the colony was
Gabriel Bernon, a Huguenot who had rank and
riches in the old world, and land was given to every
settler.

Andrew Sigourney (801) and his family were early in Oxford, and he is often mentioned in the earliest annals of the place.

In 1693, as constable, so-called, he did the duties of grand juryman, sheriff, and tax-collector. In 1694 he was ordered to collect a tax of £8, 6s., assessed upon the colony which had been exempt for four years after its settlement. He however, addressed to the governor and council a petition which was read Oct. 16, 1694. He said, in substance, " We cannot pay. The Indians appeared several times. We were obliged to garrison ourselves for three months. Our crops and hay were ruined, etc., etc." This tax and several others after it amounting to £33, 6s., were remitted.

Mr. Sigourney with his wife and five children, three boys and two girls, had their home near the French Fort on Mayo's hill, something over a mile south-east of Oxford plain. In 1693, Dec. 5, he made an affidavit protesting against the sale of Rum to Indians (Baird II, p. 273). The original of this paper is in the hands of Peter Butler (67) Quincy, Mass.

The Huguenot fort was built with a stone rampart, and with towers projecting at alternate corners. It commands a beautiful outlook over more than one township. By some strange chance it remained nearly intact for almost two centuries, when it was bought by a Huguenot society, and a granite monument with appropriate inscriptions reared beside it. Water in its well is still unfailing. The site of the powder-magazine, and barrack fire-place is still evident.

In 1696, Aug. 25, Indians surprised the settlement. Susan Sigourney (802) had married John Johnson, and had three children, André, Pierre, and Marie. All three and her husband were killed, the colony was broken up and the Sigourneys returned to Boston.

FIRST GENERATION.

801. Andrew Sigourney[1], m. Charlotte Pairau. He d. 1727, April 16.

Their children were :

802. Susannah, m. John Johnson.

803. Peter[1].

804. Charlotte, m. Peter Holman or Holton, 1719, May 26. (?)

805. Andrew[2], b. 1673, m. Mary Germaine.

806. Bartholemew, baptized 1682.

Susannah Sigourney (804) m. 1700, April 18, as her second husband her cousin Daniel Johonnot.

SECOND GENERATION.

Andrew Sigourney[2] (805) m. Mary Germaine. She had a sister six years older than herself, whose husband was Paix Cazneau.

Their children were :

807 Andrew[3], b. 1702, Jan. 30.

808. Susannah[2], b. 1704, Dec. 27, m. Martin
Brimmer, b. 1697, Osten, Germany.

809. Peter[2], b. 1706, March 1, d. 1738.

810. Mary[1], b. 1709, Aug. 1, m. John Baker
b. Guernsey, d. 1774.

811. Charles[1], b. 1711, April 27.

812. Anthony[1], b. 1713, Aug. 17.

813. Daniel[1], b. 1715, Nov. 17.

814. Rachel, b. 1718, March 5, d. before 1736.

815. Hannah[1], b. 1719, Feb. 27, m. Samuel Dexter, b. 1726, d. 1784.

THIRD GENERATION.

Andrew Sigourney[3] (807) m. Mary Ronchon.
He d. 1762.

Their children who grew up were :

816. Mary[2], b. 1735.

817. John Ronchon, b. 1740.

818. Elizabeth[1], b. 1743.

819. Susannah[3], b. 1744.

820. Charles[2], b. 1748.

821. Hannah[2], b. 1754.

Anthony Sigourney (812) m. Mary Waters, of
Salem. A bit of silk brocade that has come to me as
an heir-loom was from her wedding dress in 1740.

Their children were :

822. Mary[3] b. 1741-2, March 23, m. James Butler. (25)

823. Susannah[4], b. 1743, Jan. 11, d. young.

824. Peter[3], b. 1745, Dec. 8, m. 1769, May 30,
Celia Loring.

The second wife of Anthony Sigourney (12) was
Elizabeth Breed.

Their children were :

825. Anthony[2], b. 1751, May 12.

826. Andrew[4], b. 1752, Nov. 30. See 875.

Daniel Sigourney (813) m. Mary Varney.

Their children who grew up were :

827. Mary[1], b. 1736.

828. Andrew[4], b. 1738.

829. James, b. 1741.

830. Charles[3], b. 1744.

The second wife of Daniel Sigourney (813) was
Joanna Tileston.

Their children who grew up were :

831. Joanna, b. 1750.

832. Jane Poole, b. 1751.

833. Elisha, b. 1753.

834. Susanna[4], b. 1754.

835. Sarah[1], b. 1758.

836. Mary Ann[1], b. 1759.

Andrew Sigourney[3] (807) was a distiller and also
a sea captain. In the Boston *Weekly Journal*, of
April 6, 1728, I read : " Andrew Segarney cleared
for the West Indies." On one voyage was so near

starving that he ate his shoes and other things less palateable. He was always afterwards scrupulous never to waste a crumb of bread. He perished at sea. The morning when he last sailed, his cousin Mary (822) seeing him through a window, hurried to the door for a farewell, but could see him no more. She looked on his disappearance as ominous. On his death his widow Mary, "was approbated as as a retailer of rum and other spirits," during the remainder of the year for which he had been licens-ed. (R. C., No. 147, p 232.) In 1758 in July, twen-ty beds had been carried to his house as a Public House (p. 69) for the use of the King's troops then in town. (*Ibid*, p. 90.)

FOURTH GENERATION.

Andrew Sigourney (828) m. Ann Hammett.

Their children were :

850. Mary[5], b. 1764.

851. Andrew[6], b. 1766.

852. Daniel[2], b. 1769.

John R. Sigourney (817) m. Eunice Kidder.

Of their nine children only :

853. Mary[6], lived, to marry Nathaniel Dearborn, 1807.

James Sigourney (829) m. Mary Hammett.

854. Their dau. Mary[7], b. 1761. m. Peter Le Mer-cier.

Peter Sigourney (824) m. Celia Loring.
855, 856, 857. Of their children, Peter[1], John
Baker and Anthony[3], died at sea and unm.
858. Celia, b. 1770, Feb. 25, m. —— Williston,
and died 1854, in Roxbury, Mass.
859. James Butler, d. 1813, July 14.
No. 859 commanded U. S. schooner *Asp*. His
vessel was overpowered on the Potomac. He and
all but two in his crew of twenty were killed. Boston *Gazette*, Aug. 9, 1813.

Charles Sigourney (830) m. Sarah Frazer.
Their children who grew up were :
860. Charles[4], b. 1788, July 21.
861. Henry[1], b. 1783, July 25.

His children by second wife Mary Greenleaf, who
lived to marry were :
862. Elizabeth Parsons.
863. Mary.[8]
864. Ann Pearson.
865. Jane Carter[1].

Anthony Sigourney (825) m. Ruth Chase.
Their children were :
866. Anthony[4], b. 1775.
867. Ruth, b. 1777.
868. Andrew[7], b. 1779.
869. Elizabeth[2], b. 1781.
870. Charles[5], b. 1784.
871. Peter[5], b. 1786.
872. Sarah[2], b. 1789.

873. John, b. 1792.

His second wife's maiden name was Phillips.

Their child was :

874. Daniel P.[1], b. 1804.

Andrew Sigourney (826) 1787, m. Elizabeth Wolcott. She b. 1761, July 19, d. 1829, March 20. He d. 1838, April 16. Elizabeth was dau. of Josiah and Isabella Wolcott. (See Wolcott *Memorial*, p. 200.) Isabella was dau. of Rev. John Campbell.

Their children were :

875. William, b. 1788.

876. Elizabeth[3], b. 1789.

877. Clarissa, b. 1791.

878. Martin, b. 1793.

879. Susannah[6]. b. 1797.

880. Andrew[8], b. 1799, m. Lucy Butler (62) and (138).

881. Mary[9].

FIFTH GENERATION.

Andrew Sigourney (851) m. Sally Barker.

882. Andrew[9], their only child b. 1795, died young.

His second wife was Elizabeth Williams.

Their children who grew up were :

883. Eliza Ann, b. 1798.

884. John Cathcart, b. 1800.

885. Sarah Barker, b. 1802.

Daniel Sigourney (852) m. Martha Williams.

Their children were :

886. Daniel Andrew, b. 1800.

887. Her ry Howell Williams.

888. Martha Ann.

Anthony Sigourney (866) m. Betsey Gloyd.

Their children were:

889. Alanson, b. 1809.

890. Mary Ann[2], b. 1811.

891. James M., b. 1813.

892. William H., b. 1815.

893. Polly P., b. 1817.

894. Betsey, b. 1819.

Charles Sigourney (860) m. Jane Carter.

Their children were :

895. Charles Henry, b. 1811.

896. Elizabeth Carter, b. 1813.

897. Jane Carter[2], b. 1815.

The second wife of Charles Sigourney (860) was Lydia Huntley.

Their children were :

898. Mary Huntley, b. 1828, Aug. 3, m. Rev.
       Francis T. Russell.

899. Andrew Maximilian, b. 1830. July 11, d.
       1850, June 24.

Andrew Sigourney (868) m. Hannah Stevens.

Their children were :

900. Frederick, b. 1810.

901. Amanda M., b. 1815.

Henry Sigourney (861) m. Margaret M. Barker.

Their children were :

902. Henry[2], b. 1831, m. Amelia Rives, Albemarle Co., d. 1873, Dec., wrecked on *Ville de Havre.*

903. Margaret, b. 1833, m. 1855, W. C. Otis, N. Y.

Charles Sigourney (870) m. Sally French.

Among their children were :

904. Diantha.

905. Charles M.

906. Andrew[10].

907. John H.

908. Joseph W.

909. Anthony W

Peter Sigourney (71) m Wealthy Bates.

Their children were :

910. Louise[1], b. 1814.

911. William[2], b. 1815.

912. Caroline, b. 1818.

913. Andrew[11], b. 1820.

914. Peter[6], b. 1822.

915. Anthony[3], b. 1824.

916. Orrin, b. 1827.

917. Sarah[3], b. 1829.

918. Addison, b. 1832.

John Sigourney (73) m. Clarissa Caldwell.
Their children were :
919. Louisa², b. 1820.
920. Vilmina, b. 1826.
921. Sarah E., b. 1827.
Martin Sigourney (78) m. Susan Morgan.
Their children were :
922. Charles Andrew, b. 1823.
923. George William, b. 1826.

SIXTH GENERATION.

Daniel A. Sigourney (86) m. Harriot Davis.
Their children were :
924. Daniel³, b. 1825.
925. Harriot, b. 1832.
926. Elizabeth⁴, b. 1835.
John C. Sigourney (84) m. Martha Ann Cargill.
Their child was :
927. Andrew John C., b. 1824, m. Alicia Ferguson, of Baltimore.
Daniel P. Sigourney (874) m. E. Jane Cary.
Their children were : .
928. Thaddeus W.
929. William A.
930. Mary J.
931. Daniel P.²
932. Elizabeth S.

933. Charles F.

934. Abram C.

935. Jacob L.

936. Hannah M.

937. Winfield S.

Henry H. W. Sigourney (887) m. Harriot A. Williams.

Their children were :

938. Henry H. W.^{2}, b. 1832.

939. Harriot A., b. 1834.

940. Eliza W., b. 1838.

941. Thomas W., b. 1840, d. 1853, Dedham.

Charles A. Sigourney (922) m. Sarah Hutchinson. Their children were :

942. Charles H.

943. Isabella H.

Andrew J. C. Sigourney (927) m. Alicia Ferguson. Their children were :

944. Andrew^{12}, b. 1851.

945. Thomas, b. 1852.

Henry Sigourney (902) m. Amelia Louise Rives. Their son :

946. Henry^3, b. 1855, Feb. 27, perished 1873, Dec., on *Ville de Havre.*

APPENDIX AND CORRECTIONS.

The statement on page 18 that Stephen Butler petitions for release from imprisonment was copied from the index to documents in the Boston State House, as I hold it the duty of a faithful chronicler to extenuate nothing. I have, however, examined the petition itself, and thus discovered that it was not made by my ancestor at all, but by Stephen Barrett whose name was erroneously written Butler in the index.

In like manner the James Butler mentioned on p. 26, as in prison for selling liquor is proved by his petition not to have been my ancestor, but a foreign immigrant, and a man already in business when my James Butler was no more than nine years old.

Benjamin Butler (4) on p. 24, is stated to have married Susanna Gallup. Possibly the husband of this Susanna may have been John Butler, born 1653, son of John Butler, haberdasher.—*Suffolk Deeds*, vol. 28, p. 21.

Thomas, son of Mary Shepcot (p. 26) was a retailer. In 1745, Sept. 17, his widow was his administrator.

The Elizabeth Butler (p. 25, No. 16), who married Ephraim Savage may have been the widow of Peter Butler.

James Butler, stated on p. 34 to have gone to Halifax, is believed to have returned, lived some years in Sutton, as well as to have died and been buried there.

The landlord (p. 38) of the Kennebec fugitives, it has been ascertained, was of Boston origin and probably their kinsman. In 1718 John Butler of Boston sold Butler's Row to his brother Peter, and is supposed to have removed to Maine. William of Arrowsic was his son or grandson. The French fusil (p. 38) is still in the possession of Peter Butler (67).

The account of the Sigourney family, on p. 136, is in some points at variance with the traditions of the race. According to these relations the family home was in Rochelle, and their occupation distilling, just as afterwards in Boston. They are also said to have brought away a great quantity of household stuff. Chairs, tables, etc., of French fashion, have been handed down among their descendants from the first generations. It may be that chattels, of which these heirlooms are survivals, had been secretly put on board a vessel at Rochfort, and so nothing was left to be confiscated. The family may also have been engaged both in distilling and in shoemaking. There is no proof that the Sigourneys came (p. 127) on the *first* vessel which brought Huguenots in great destitution. They may have come later and have brought property with them. A large bundle of manuscripts in French which had been handed down from the earliest Sigourney immigrants, but had never been examined by any one acquainted with the language, deposited in the safe of Peter Butler in State street, Boston. These documents which would probably have thrown much light on the Sigourney ancestry perished in the great fire November 1872.

(p. 62). Other children of James D. Butler (No. 44) were :

Mary, m. Edmund Roberts.
Adeline, m. Albert More. She d. 1847, Aug. 21.
Peter, d. Vera Cruz.

Franklin.
Willard.
James D , m. Nancy Burdick.
(p. 67) Another son of Eliza Butler Olney was
Frederick.
Mary Lilley (p. 69, No. 160) d. in Brookline, June
26, 1888.
The first child of C. C. Higgins and Sarah his
wife (p. 69) was b. 1888, July 23, 8 P. M.
(p. 74). To children of Peter Butler Olney add
Sigourney Butler, b. 1888, Feb. 22.
The children of Eben Sutton Stevens (p. 67) and
Gertrude Olney his wife, b. 1846, Dec. 11, m. 1872,
Sept. 10, were :
Gertrude Olney, b. 1873. Nov. 15.
They have adopted two children of their Camp-
bell kindred. Their home is Quinebaug, Conn.
David Owen, mentioned (p. 93), had come to Salis-
bury from Lebanon.
The children of Samuel L. Harris (p. 110) were :
Roderick, b. 1838, Aug. 25.
Ellen, b. 1839.
Laura N., b. 1840, Nov. 15.
Charles, b. 1842, July 18.
Elizabeth. b. 1844, Nov. 13.
Emily B., b. 1846, June 27.
Ida N., b. 1849, Feb. 4.
Adeline, b. 1851, Feb. 14.
William Stone, b. 1854, July 14.
His home is Clifton, Holt Co., Nebraska. His
wife d. 1873, Nov. 18.
In reference to the statements concerning insanity
on p. 81, it ought to be added that the derangement
of David (321) was a clear result of his being injured
by a door which fell upon him, that Prentiss (332)
suffered from pre-natal influences, and that Mary's .
difficulty (327) was melancholic hypochondria.

ERRATA.

Page 9 line 12, for General read Genealogical.
Page 12 line 5, for ate read late.
Page 24 last line, for Blower read Blomer.
Page 35 line 10, strike out 4 D.
Page 61 line 7, for 1848 read 1888.
Page 62 line 5, for 1818 read 1816.
Page 63 line 2, for (53) read (52).
Page 63 line 7, for (52) read (48).
Page 67 No. 152, for Isabelle read Isabel.
Page 66 No. 138. for Lloyd read Lhoyd.
Page 68 No. 154, for Ann read Annie.
Page 69. for Artemeisia read Artemisia.
Page 84 line 23, for incapaciated read incapacitated.
Page 86 line 7, for Fansworth read Farnsworth.
Page 91 line 16, for 1754-63 read 1745.
Page 145 line 8, for memoral read Memorial.

Many genealogists confine their research to persons bearing their own surnames. My aim on the other hand, would be to trace the lineage of all persons, no matter how manifold the names, from whom I am descended. I would not so stick to the name as to miss the nature. My children are half Bates, one fourth Harris, one-eighth Sigourney, one-sixteenth Davie, one-thirty-second Eustiss, one-sixty-fourth Newcomb. Accordingly, I wish I could trace back all those families to their origin, and trust my genealogical successors may be actuated by a similar spirit and accomplish what I could only attempt.

INDEXES.

A book without an index resembles a clock-face without hands to show either seconds, minutes or hours. The word index means a *forefinger*. As a man who has lost a forefinger is maimed and mutilated, so is every book which lacks an index.

I. PERSONS SURNAMED BUTLER.

Figures refer to *numbers* not pages.

II. PERSONS SURNAMED BATES.

Figures refer to *numbers* not pages.

319 Abigail[1].
324 Abigail[2].
320 Abby.
326 Adeline.
337 Agnes.
322 Anna[1].
334 Anna[2].
344 Arthur Lee.

311 Bathsheba.
305 Benjamin.
308 Caleb.
350 Charles How.
300 Clement[1].
302 Clement[2].
312 Clement[3].

318 Daniel.
321 David.

313 Eleazar.
343 Elizabeth.
342 Frank Cornelius.
309 Hannah[1].
328 Hannah[2].
301 James.
325 Jane[1].
335 Jane[2].
345 Jane.
331 John Codman.
304 Joseph[1].
307 Joseph[2].
310 Joshua[1].
314 Joshua[2].
315 Joshua[3].
317 Joshua[4].
330 Joshua[5].

347 Kate Lee.

338 Maria.
327 Mary.
320 Paul.
323 Phineas.
332 Prentiss.

393 Rachel.

306 Samuel[1].
346 Samuel Lee.
336 Samuel Worcester[1].
349 Samuel Worcester[2].

348 Waldron.
333 William.

316 Zealous.

III. PERSONS SURNAMED HARRIS.

Figures refer to *numbers* not pages.

472 Abigail[1].
483 Abigail[2].
570 Abner.
556 bis. Adeline.
236 Agnes Butler.
625 Alfred Jennings.
550 Alvan B.
487 Anne.

736 Caroline Emma.
737 Celia Ellen[1].
227 Celia Elizabeth
528 Charles[1].
608 Charles[2].
688 Charles Butler.
647 Charles Gerald.
230 Charles Leonard.
669 Charles Salter.
517 Chloe
583 Chloe Lucretia.

731 Clara Funke.
520 Christina.
638 bis. Clara E.
674 Clarissa Dell.
620 bis. Cornelia.
461 Daniel[1].
463 Daniel[2].
475 Daniel[3].
480 Daniel[4].
526 Deborah.

606 Edgar.
625 bis. Edward.
233 Edward Kirk.
621 bis. Eliza.
466 Elizabeth[1].
474 Elizabeth[2].
478 Elizabeth[3].
493 Elizabeth[4]
499 Elizabeth[5].

509 Elizabeth[6].
557 Elizabeth[7].
554 bis. Elizabeth.
564 bis. Elizabeth
571 bis. Elizabeth.
569 bis. Ellen.
494 Eunice.

667 Fanny Loraine.
597 Frederick.
232 Fred'k Lement

582 George.
228 George Bacon
594 George Samuel.
486 Gilbert.

471 Hannah[1].
495 Hannah[2].
521 Hannah[3].
604 Hannah[4].

585 Harriet Newell.
627 bis. Henry Clay.

555 Ida.
488 Israel[1].
505 Israel[2].
512 Israel[3].
568 bis. Israel[4].
623 bis. Israel Hopkins.
489 James[1].
569 James[2].
580 James[3].
596 James[4].
553 James Butler.
642 bis. James Ramsey.
470 John[1].
451 John[2].
497 John[3].
502 John[4].
504 John[5].
508 John[6].
525 John[7].
549 John[8].
235 John Francis.
485 Joshua.
612 John Kellogg.
638 bis. Clara E.
639 bis. John L.
623 bis. John Porter.
464 Joseph[1].
476 Joseph[2].
484 Joseph[3].
484 bis. Joseph.
514 Joseph[4].
575 Joseph[5].
624 bis Joseph[6].
645 Josephine Lucretia.
531 Julia Ann.

692 Katharine.
738 Katharine McClure.

646 Kate Mary.
548 Laura[1].
578 Laura[2].
584 Laura Bethiah.
626 bis. Laura E.
574 Laura Eliza.
593 Leonard G.
492 Lois[1].
516 Lois[2].
522 Lois[3].
571 Lois Noble.
577 Louisa.
576 Lucretia.
579 Lydia Ann.

624 bis. Margaret.
462 Mary[1].
473 Mary[2].
566 bis. Mary[3].
581 Mary[4].
587 Mary[5].
641 bis. Mary Adelaide.
690 Mary Eliza
231 Mary Germaine.
735 Mary Turner.
595 Michael.
668 Minnie Field.
479 Miriam.
481 Moses.
482 bis. Moses, Jr.
565 bis. Nancy.
477 Patience.
555 Perry.
490 Polly.
554 Porter.

491 Rachel[1].
506 Rachel[2].
511 Rachel[3].
519 Rachel[4].
563 bis. Rachel[5].
570 bis. Rachel.
629 bis. Reuben Munger.

557 bis Roderick.
524 Rosalie[1].
605 Rosalie[2].
689 Rosalie[3].

507 Samuel[1].
513 Sameul[2].
523 Samuel[3].
552 Samuel[4].
607 Samuel[5].
691 Samuel Arthur.
572 Samuel Noble.
467 Sarah[1].
468 Sarah[2].
510 Sarah[3].
551 Sarah[4].
567 bis. Sarah[5].
234 Sarah Butler.
586 Sarah Knowles.
689 Sarah Rosalie.
496 Seth.
498 Silas.
530 Stephen V. R.
229 Susan Ellen
640 bis. Susan Maria.
573 Susan Willard.

450 Thomas[1].
452 Thomas[2].
465 Thomas[3].
482 Thomas[4].
603 Thomas G.
739 Thomas Stewart.
503 Timothy[1].
515 Timothy[2].
527 Timothy[3].

737 Walter Stewart.
453 William[1].
469 William[2].
483 bis. William[3].
556 William[4].
622 bis. William[5].
558 bis. William.
529 Zina.

158   BUTLER GENEALOGY.

IV. PERSONS SURNAMED SIGOURNEY.

Figures refer to *numbers* not pages.

934 Abram C.
918 Addison.
889 Alanson.
891 Andrew[1].
805 Andrew[2].
807 Andrew[3].
826 Andrew[4].
828 Andrew[5].
851 Andrew[6].
868 Andrew[7].
880 Andrew[8].
882 Andrew[9].
906 Andrew[10].
913 Andrew[11].
944 Andrew[12].
927 Andrew J. C.
899 Andrew Maximilian.
864 Ann Pearson.
812 Anthony[1].
825 Anthony[2].
857 Anthony[3].
866 Anthony[4].
915 Anthony[5].
909 Anthony W.

806 Bartholomew.
894 Betsey.

912 Caroline.
858 Celia.
811 Charles[1].
820 Charles[2].
830 Charles[3].
860 Charles[4].
870 Charles[5].
922 Charles Andrew.
933 Charles F.
942 Charles H.
895 Charles Henry.
905 Charles M.
804 Charlotte.
877 Clarissa.

813 Daniel[1].
832 Daniel[2].
924 Daniel[3].

886 Daniel Andrew.
874 Daniel S.[1]
931 Daniel S.[2]
904 Diantha.
833 Elisha.
883 Eliza Ann.
940 Eliza W.
818 Elizabeth[1].
869 Elizabeth[2].
876 Elizabeth[3].
926 Elizabeth[4].
896 Elizabeth Carter.
862 Elizabeth Parsons.
932 Elizabeth S.
923 George William.
815 Hannah[1].
821 Hannah[2].
936 Hannah M.
925 Harriot.
939 Harriot A.
861 Henry[1].
902 Henry[2].
946 Henry[3].
887 Henry H. W[1].
938 Henry H. W[2].
943 Isabella H.
935 Jacob L.
829 James.
859 James Butler.
891 James M.
865 Jane Carter[1].
897 Jane Carter[2].
832 Jane Poole.
831 Joanna.
873 John.
856 John Baker.
884 John Cathcart.
907 John H
817 John Ronchon.
903 Joseph W.
910 Louisa.
919 Louisa[2].

903 Margaret.
888 Martha Ann.
878 Martin.
810 Mary[1].
816 Mary[2].
822 Mary[3].
827 Mary[4].
850 Mary[5].
853 Mary[6].
854 Mary[7].
863 Mary[8].
881 Mary[9].
836 Mary Ann[1].
890 Mary Ann[2].
898 Mary Huntley.
930 Mary J.
916 Orrin.
803 Peter[1].
809 Peter[2].
824 Peter[3].
855 Peter[4].
871 Peter[5].
914 Peter[6].
893 Polly P,
814 Rachel.
835 Sarah[1].
872 Sarah[2].
917 Sarah[3].
885 Sarah Barker
921 Sarah E.
802 Susannah[1].
808 Susannah[2].
819 Susannah[3].
823 Susannah[4].
834 Susannah[5].
928 Thaddeus W
915 Thomas.
941 Thomas W.
920 Vilmina.
875 William[1].
911 William[2].
929 William A.
892 William H.
937 Winfield S.

V. INDEX TO ALL OTHER NAMES.

Figures refer to *pages*.

www.ingramcontent.com/pod-product-compliance
Lightning Source LLC
Chambersburg PA
CBHW022358020726

47500CB00002B/337